# Sacred Trust

## An Army / Navy Love Story

### Mary Ellen Cortellini

F·C·GORDON

Merriam Press Historical Fiction 9

First Edition published in 2013 by the Merriam Press

First Edition

Copyright © 2013 by Mary Ellen Cortellini
Book design by Mary Ellen Cortellini and Ray Merriam
Additional material copyright of named contributors.

All rights reserved.
No part of this book may be used or reproduced in any manner whatsoever
without written permission, except in the case of brief quotations embodied in
critical articles or reviews.

WARNING
The unauthorized reproduction or distribution of this copyrighted work is
illegal. Criminal copyright infringement, including infringement without
monetary gain, is investigated by the FBI and is punishable by up to five years
in federal prison and a fine of $250,000.

The views expressed are solely those of the author.

ISBN 978-1484993361
Merriam Press #HF9-P
Library of Congress Control Number: 2013940710

This work was designed, produced, and published in
the United States of America by the

MERRIAM
PRESS
133 Elm Street Suite 3R
Bennington VT 05201

E-mail: ray@merriam-press.com
Web site: merriam-press.com

The Merriam Press publishes new manuscripts on historical subjects, especially
military history and with an emphasis on World War II, as well as reprinting
previously published works, including reports, documents, manuals, articles
and other materials on historical topics.

*On the Cover*
*Off Duty, courtesy of Gallery Graphics.*

# Dedication

To my Family

# The Making of an Army Screenplay by a Navy Captain's Wife

_____

Writers Guild of America, west #1146105

Plot Point:

"A plot point is any incident, episode, or event that "hooks" into the action and spins it around into another direction."

Syd Field
(Noted Screenplay writer)

Mr. and Mrs. Bernard Murphy
request the honour of your presence
at the marriage of their daughter
Mary Ellen
to
Louis Joseph Cortellini
Ensign, United States Navy
Friday, the fifteenth of August
nineteen hundred and eighty
at one o'clock
St. Joseph Chapel
College of the Holy Cross
Worcester, Massachusetts

Photos courtesy of Andrew Castaldi

"The day I moved into "Fort Rosecrans" was a plot point in my life. Little did I know when I married an Ensign in the Navy 27 years ago, that I would end up writing a screenplay proposal about the United States Army."

—Mary Ellen Cortellini

CDR Anderson,

I was given your name and number by Jack to contact you about my idea for writing a screenplay for a future movie. I have done two years of research on the former Army post of Fort Rosecrans in San Diego at the turn of the century. (My husband and I are residents in the 100-year-old Army-built quarters overlooking the entrance to San Diego Bay.) My work now fills an entire room with documents from the San Diego Historical Society, Laguna Archives, Washington DC Archives, the US Army Military History Institute, the Special Collections Library at West Point and so much more. These official documents, combined with the newspaper articles I discovered reading microfilm at the San Diego Public Library, tell the story of the personal and "human" side of life here on the post between 1902-1905. The story is a beautiful mix of military and local San Diego history. And I know it's a cliché to say, but "it really does have all the elements of a great movie!!!" The tale unfolds during the buildup of the fort including officers quarters, barracks, and hospital, etc. The coast artillery and their big guns, military weddings and protocol and social customs, politics, high society, picnics, parades, fireworks, and gala events at the Hotel Del, offices on Fifth avenue in the Gaslamp quarter ... you name it, it's got it ... and it's good!! Piecing all of the documents and photos together, including the contacts I've made with descendants of the men and women stationed here in 1904, has brought the story and its remarkable cast of characters back to life!! And I haven't even mentioned the modern-day Fort Rosecrans soldiers who are still here 100 years later and their incredible history!!! ... Unsung heroes who lost three friends in Afghanistan fighting the war on terror after 9/11 and just returning from a 7-month deployment to Kuwait. This is the brave unit of the Army's 710th Ordnance Company (EOD). After "adopting them" and raising money for a proper homecoming, they surprised me with a plaque and knighted me an honorary lifetime member of the Explosive Ordnance Disposal Fraternity. Not too shabby for a 24 year career Navy wife!! I am overwhelmed by the amount of history and information I have unearthed, but I am determined to get this story out there. Please come see this place and you will understand the value of a film highlighting both Army and Navy history and its potential inspirational value in support of our troops today. It's been an incredible journey but I can't rest or stop until I pay tribute to the soldiers responsible for these magnificent homes and to those from the 710th who died for me in Kandahar in 2002. Looking forward to hearing from you...

Sincerely,

Mary Ellen Cortellini
151 North Sylvester Road
San Diego, CA

*San Diego military historian Karen Scanlon and I met with
Bob Anderson and Kathy Canham Ross
from the Army Office of Information on the 21<sup>st</sup> of September 2004.*

*They told us to go home and write a treatment and find a production company.
This published book is the final result.*

**Pitch:**

*Sacred Trust* is an epic Army/Navy love story, past and present. Based on a true story, the film takes the audience back in time to a bygone era of Army glory in San Diego at the turn of the twentieth century. It also captures the storyline of a modern-day Army couple stationed at the former post of Fort Rosecrans, now an active Navy base, one hundred years later. The two worlds unite. It is a continuum of flashbacks connecting the past to the present from the perspective of two military spouses.

The film brings the first occupants of Officers' Row back to life while at the same time highlighting their young Army successors, fighting the global war on terror after 9/11, a century later. The parallel stories of love, loss, and heroism are timeless and classic.

**Logline:**

*Sacred Trust* is the story of Alle Brighton, a newly-wed military wife who discovers a tale of love and heroism in a journal of forgotten memoirs that transports her to a bygone era of Army Glory in San Diego at the turn of the twentieth century. When Alle's husband becomes the only survivor of a tragedy that kills three men from his Army unit in Afghanistan shortly after 9/11, it inspires her to fight for the recognition of the soldiers from "Fort Rosecrans," both past and present.

**Synopsis:**

Residing in 100-year-old military quarters onboard an active Naval Submarine Base, a young military wife uncovers a bygone era of Army glory in San Diego at the turn of the twentieth century.

*Sacred Trust* brings the first occupants of "Officers' Row" back to life during the heyday of the former Army post of Fort Rosecrans. The forgotten soldiers had slipped silently into the shadows, only to be rediscovered, a century later.

*Sacred Trust* vividly captures and seamlessly integrates the current war on terror and an historic romance between handsome West Point graduate, Captain Ernest Scott, and San Diego debutante Ella von Engel. When Ella chooses this young Army officer over her childhood sweetheart and Naval Academy graduate, Lieutenant Tom Windsor, a rivalry begins. Jealousy and tensions mount throughout their military careers, colliding in one pivotal moment of historic proportions.

During an early morning, pre-deployment start-up, two boilers explode aboard the Navy gunboat USS *Bennington*. Clouds of black smoke and steam and the scent of death rise over San Diego's waterfront. Bodies are spewed over the length of the ship and into the harbor. The Army's role in the aftermath of the explosion is significant, and has been overlooked for one hundred years...

Inspired by a true story, *Sacred Trust* is a unique film about one woman's fight to tell an Army story in a modern-day Navy town. The characters are interwoven throughout the magnificent social events that took place in San Diego at the turn of the 20th century, highlighting the beauty, elegance, and military pageantry in the city. The settings overlook the beautiful entrance to San Diego Bay, the majestic island of Coronado, and the sparkling blue waters of the Pacific Ocean. Men in uniform accompany ladies to formal balls at the opulent seaside resort, Hotel del Coronado. There are yachting excursions to the boardwalk at Tent City, picnics at the Point Loma lighthouse, fireworks above Glorietta Bay, Friday night hops at the new Army post...and in an instant, the resonance of terror, and one of the deadliest peacetime disasters in the history of the Navy.

The parallel stories of the Soldiers of Fort Rosecrans 1902-1905 and their successors of 2002-2005, culminate in the fulfillment of a 100 year-old historic Army/Navy promise.

The film begins in a stately old colonial home in New York in 1915. There is a young girl crying at her mother's bedside. The figure in the bed is pale, weak, and dying. The little girl sobs, "Don't leave me mother, you'll be better soon, you'll see...Please don't go, I need you... I'm all alone. Father is gone and I have no one. Please, please, mother...I beg you, don't leave me."

The woman, barely strong enough to speak, whispers to her beautiful child, "There is something I must tell you. The man who raised you, was not your real father...It is time for you to know the truth"...And taking her last breath, we hear the words, "Hero, San Diego," and then she is gone.

In the next scene we "fast forward" to 2001 and find a couple snuggling in bed, early in the morning, in their expensive (yuppie) NYC high-rise condo. The alarm clock goes off. The wife wants her husband to stay in bed with her and take the day off. Of course he says he can't (busy brokerage firm, caught up in the corporate rat race) and promises to make it up to her. The wife tries to coax him to stay home, puts the pressure on, but just ends up making him late for the office. He jumps in a cab and directs the driver downtown to the World Trade Center...

After he leaves, the wife is in the kitchen having coffee, talking on the phone complaining to her girlfriends about her husband's work schedule, and turns on the TV. She begins to hear the morning news reports, turns up the volume, and watches as the planes are heading for the Twin Towers of the WTC... The United States has been attacked and the nation is held captive in fear.

The husband, who thankfully never made it into work on time that day, returns to active duty in the Army.

Scott Brighton was on the verge of becoming a very successful stockbroker. His father-in-law set him up with a good job, which meant a nice home and a safe life. He had left the Army where he had a promising career in the dangerous world of Explosive Ordnance Disposal and he wonders if he made the right decision. It seemed right at the time. He'd served his country, and it's hard to have a wife and family in the Army. He wasn't about to lose Allison who didn't want any part of the military. She was settled in her career as a certified financial planner with a lucrative position in Westchester County. But to Scott, something was missing.

September 11, 2001 changed everything. Scott signs up for active duty once again and is recommissioned. He receives orders to the 710th Ordnance Company, Explosive Ordnance Disposal (EOD), located on the former Army post of Fort Rosecrans in San Diego, CA. The area is now home to the Naval Submarine Base, located on the peninsula of Point Loma.

*The Headquarters of the Soldiers of the 710th Ordnance Company (EOD). This building was the old post bakery completed in 1904.*

But Alle is angry: at the terrorists, the world events, and the Army. And she fears for her husband's life. She will accompany Scott to his new duty station, but is definitely not happy about it. Neither are her parents or her tight-knit group of girlfriends from work.

She commiserates with them by phone, oblivious to the fact that her words portray a shallow, self-centered, materialistic young woman caught up in the web of corporate "perks." And those horrible wives' clubs!" she quips, "Can you imagine me with big hair, pearls, and white gloves?"

Alle's stress is made worse by the fact that Scott, although he tries unsuccessfully to hide it, is excited at the prospect of doing something meaningful again in the company of fellow warriors. He packs up his duffel bag with uniforms, listening to loud rock 'n' roll music, while Alle steams. She 'warns' him that he'd better take some leave time to help her during the move and reminds him of the true meaning of EOD: EveryOne's Divorced. The hardships of being a military spouse are all too real now, and she has many doubts about her decision of leaving her family and friends behind in New York.

The moving van is parked outside the quarters along Officers' Row overlooking the Pacific Ocean and the entrance to San Diego Bay. Captain Scott Brighton reports to work. He is excited about being back in the elite and highly-trained community of Army EOD. And he is happy for the reunion with his buddies, Jake, Bill, and Toby, from previous companies. They tease him about giving up corporate America to "get paid to blow things up." That evening when he gets home, he brings the news of his unit's orders, by Presidential directive, to fly to Afghanistan. The mission: to work with the Special Forces "A" team in the search for Osama bin Laden and the Al Qaeda terrorists responsible for the recent attacks. With less than 24 hours notice, Scott Brighton and all the men and women of the 710th, must ship out.

The couple spends only one night together in their new home. They lay in sleeping bags on the enclosed front porch, too fatigued and distracted by the impending deployment to locate and unpack the bed linens in the shipment of their household goods. The next morning, contractors and painters from the housing office are running in and out, putting the final touches on the recently restored historic properties. They pick up their supplies for the final walkthrough inspection. The men are in a hurry and anxious to go.

Alle is frustrated by all the chaos and while attempting to close a stuck drawer in the dining room's built-in china closet, she jams her finger. Tucked away behind the drawer, Alle discovers an old, yellowed package. She removes the drawer completely to further investigate the bundle of papers, wrapped in twine. She plans to put the package on the fireplace mantle while she tends to her wound.

*Actual sideboard and fireplace in military quarters along Officers' Row, Fort Rosecrans.*

"Scott, who do you think these belong to?" **She removes an envelope on top and in the reflection of the mirror above the fireplace, she is surprised to see her name. Upon closer inspection, she realizes it is actually the word "ELLA" (ALLE backwards) which is handwritten across the front of it.** She nonchalantly puts the envelope, and its contents, in the pocket of her jeans, to investigate more closely at a later time.

Scott doesn't answer her previous question, his mind is focused on his trip overseas and the suspected WMD sites waiting for him and his friends on the other end. (The threat of chemical, biological, and nuclear warfare was heavy on everyone's minds at that time. These young men and women bravely answered the call and marched into the face of unknown danger, during one of the most frightening times in our nation's history. It is important to capture their extraordinary courage and the country's overwhelming patriotic sentiment.)

The couple walks out the front door and head towards the unit's small headquarters building at the end of the base. The "band of brothers" of the 710th are already packing up their gear. They are brave and young, trained, and ready to go. It is a tearful farewell for their families.

"Here's a souvenir piece of our new home to take with you," says Alle belligerently. She slips a small gold object from inside the envelope in her pocket, into Scott's pocket. He picks up his duffel bag and Alle adds, "Hope it makes you think of me as I'm hanging all the pictures on the walls by myself!" "Get over here girl and give me a hug," says Scott. They embrace.

It is extremely hard to say that last goodbye. Alle clings to Scott. She doesn't know in her heart if she will ever see him again, it feels like a day of mourning. A good cry is the next order of business.

Alle walks back towards her home along Officers' Row, holding back tears, when she bumps into her neighbor Caroline Fletcher. She is a Navy wife whose husband Mike, a helicopter pilot, is already overseas. Caroline welcomes Alle to the "Navy" neighborhood and they immediately hit it off. They stand outside for awhile on the expansive front lawn and chat. The ocean view brings a sense of warmth to Alle's uneasy spirit. The homes are magnificent and she finally has a moment to appreciate their exquisite architecture.

EXT. ALLE'S HOME ALONG OFFICERS' ROW 2001 – DAY

Alle is a brand new Army wife. Her husband Scott, an EOD soldier, has just left on deployment to Afghanistan, soon after 9/11. Saying goodbye is a disorienting feeling and that first day seems interminable. Because Alle doesn't know in her heart if she will ever see her husband again, it feels like a day of mourning.

The couple just said their goodbyes and Alle is still teary-eyed as she walks back to her military quarters on base. She is by herself, feeling very alone, and very far from her family and friends in New York.

She bumps into her neighbor, Caroline Fletcher, a veteran Navy spouse with over 25 years "in the business," who makes it sound like a walk in the park, in an Erma Bombeck sort of way.

Caroline mentors Alle, giving her the lay of the land about military spouses and trying to comfort her with some tough love to get her through her husband's first deployment.

CAROLINE
Come on honey, shake it off, you'll be okay.

What's your name, sweetie?

ALLE
"Alle."

CAROLINE
Okay... "Army"...

Caroline teases her by "assigning her" this new nickname.

> Welcome to the Navy... let me tell you a few things about this place that will help you in the long run.
>
> Rule #1... we're all going through the same thing.
>
> You think you got it rough, and the girl next door's probably got it even worse. I've been in your shoes before with the 12 hour waterworks. Doesn't do you any good to sit and fret about it. Those that do, don't last long in these parts. And crying your eyes out, doesn't bring 'em home any sooner either.

Alle gives her a "this is not helping" stare.

The two women walk and stop on the expansive green lawn overlooking the sparkling blue waters of the Pacific ocean, extending into infinity.

                    CAROLINE (CONT'D)
See those helicopters going by? My husband flies those babies, mostly at night, off the decks of moving aircraft carriers.

What's your husband do?

                    ALLE
Diffuses bombs for a living.

                    CAROLINE
Sounds like we both married a couple of nutcases, huh?

Alle cracks a smile, and then, finally, laughs out loud. The two women get off to a good start.

                    CAROLINE (CONT'D)
See? We got a lot in common already "Army." Things are going to work out just fine. You'll see. The first day's the longest. Tomorrow you'll start planning the homecoming. Take it from me, it's better to pick yourself up, brush yourself off, and just keep right on going. Stiff upper lip and all that kind of thing.

You're a survivor, I can tell just by looking at you. And I know you got some stamina in you too, cause I heard you and Casanova on the porch last night.

Rule # 2, the walls got ears around here.

Both women start chuckling.

> CAROLINE
>
> What do you plan on doing with yourself while hubby's away?

> ALLE
>
> Oh, I don't know. I got a background in financial management.
>
> I'll get a handle on these boxes first, hang a few pictures on the wall, and then I'll worry about that.

> CAROLINE
>
> I'm always on the hunt for a good adventure. I'm sitting here talking to a rookie, aren't I??
>
> Wouldn't mind getting into some "Lucy and Ethel" trouble while my husband Mike's away.
>
> You in?

> ALLE
>
> I'm in.

> CAROLINE
>
> Come on Army, let's get outta here and get you something to eat.
>
> Are you old enough to drink yet?

Caroline giggles.

Once back inside in her home, and despite floor-to-ceiling cardboard boxes to attend to, it is the delicate bundle of papers sitting on the fireplace mantel that capture Alle's attention. She is drawn to them, and begins to read about another military wife who has gone before her.

As Alle starts... we hear a voice in the background. It is a young Ella von Engel and the scene flashes back to the past...

Ella describes her loving parents, her older sister Leda, younger sister Amy, and their privileged life in a wealthy, upper-class family in San Diego. Ella adores her father, Charles P. von Engel. He is a descendant of a German baron, and now a prominent businessman in the growing city of San Diego. Ella also talks fondly about her best friend Lizzy Larson and all of her debutante girlfriends in her family's influential circle. Her journal entry opens to an event that took place when Ella was seven years old. It was there that she got her first kiss from her childhood sweetheart Tom Windsor.

It is the evening of August 14, 1888, and the all-male Cuyamaca (Kwee-ya-maca) Club, the "who's who" in the city of San Diego, opens its beautiful new facility for an inaugural reception that includes refreshments and dancing. The attendees are the elite citizens, visionaries and builders of the booming "new "San Diego. Influential. Wealthy. Wanting. It is a brilliant gathering of San Diego society—"the grandest and most enjoyable social event of the season in this city. The front of the club building is brilliantly illuminated with Chinese lanterns, while the scene from within is one of dazzling beauty. The elegant draperies and curtains, and the delicately tinted walls, and superb furniture, blended well with the pretty dresses of the ladies."

The Cuyamaca Club had been established the year before as "a place to meet and talk over town affairs." The members of this organization were the pioneers and founding fathers of San Diego during an era of commercial revival; the "good ole boys" club where dreams were not realized by anyone other than the wealthy, the powerful, and the downright gutsy.

Club President Heber Ingle (Donald Trump type) loves the spotlight and greets his guests with an eager and animated handshake. His brother-in-law, Elisha Babcock, arrives with an entourage of city newcomers, guests of his grand seaside resort the Hotel del Coronado. Mr. Ingle moves across the floor to welcome retired Admiral Edward Windsor and his wife Clara. "Hello Edward, I hear your jewelry business is flourishing these days. Well done Sir. Never would have believed a crusty old sea captain like yourself could ever pull it off," he says jokingly. Mr. and Mrs. Engel join in the conversation and share words of praise for the beautiful downtown store, recently opened by Admiral Windsor after his retirement from a long and illustrious military career. The men discuss business...

Clara Windsor leans over to gossip with her close friend, Florence von Engel. Florence, Ella's mother, is the wife of the affluent, German-born 'mover and shaker' who built one of the finest residences in San Diego, bringing fresh blood to the dwindling town. Charles owns the local newspaper, a retail shop on Fifth Ave, and is the proprietor of the exclusive Horton Hotel in the city. And Florence delights in letting everyone know this. Social standing in the community means everything to this woman.

The two women chatter, comparing the soiree to "THE Mrs. Astor's" grandiose parties in Newport, Rhode Island. They frown upon their children who have escaped the care of nannies in the adjacent nursery. Clara's three young sons, Edward Jr, Jerauld, and Tom, formally dressed in blue sailor suits, romp with the three young von Engel sisters, Leda, Ella, and Amy. For a moment they negate the existence of rules and twirl in gay abandon. The mischievous boys chase and tease the girls dressed in starched pinafores, and Tom is seen pulling a large bow from the hair of seven-year old Ella. As she turns to retrieve the stolen hairpiece, Tom steals his first kiss. Ella responds, "You naughty boy!" But very soon afterwards, skipping along hand in hand, Ella turns to him, "Tom Windsor, promise me we will always be together and live happily ever after?"

[Oil on Canvas, n.d. Courtesy Schillay and Rehs, Inc., New York ©1988 New York Graphic Society]

*MAY I HAVE THIS DANCE by Alexander Mark Rossi (British, fl. 1870-1903)*

We overhear their mothers talking. They are predicting with unabashed certainty that the two children will grow up and get married one day.

While the children play, businessmen huddle in the corner and tout San Diego's climate, favorable location by the sea, benefits to health, and available real estate. They discuss the importance of bringing the military to San Diego and warn guests not to rest on one's laurels and let Los Angeles acquire the reported ten-company post, thus leaving San Diego Harbor defenseless. One gentleman, puffing on a cigar, quotes the society journal Seaport News: "Five- or six-hundred soldiers with a regimental band would not only give éclat (acclaim) to the city, but would prove a great drawing card. We will venture to say that the summer travel here would be doubled in one season. There would be gayeties of all kinds constantly…"

Night falls, and Alle can no longer see the handwritten words on the pages, and is forced to stop and search for a lamp in the unlabeled moving boxes. "One day of the deployment down," she says aloud to herself, "one day closer to the homecoming."

Things look brighter the next morning. As Alle settles into the beautiful quarters, she is captivated by Ella's journal and begins to uncover the stories of the original occupants of her incredible home. The rich history of the dwelling is revealed to her and the audience, as the story continues to unfold.

*"View from my Kitchen Window"*

*Fort Rosecrans*

*The painting was based on a photograph taken by firefighter, friend, and artist David Meza while he was stationed at Fire Station #13, Navy Base Point Loma.*

*Firefighter Meza incorporated sand from the beaches of Coronado into the painting based on the location of the historic military homes which overlook the Pacific Ocean, the entrance to San Diego Bay, Coronado, and the Hotel Del. The gift was commissioned by the Naval Spouses of HSCWINGPAC.*

This scene takes place at the United States Military Academy at West Point, New York. It is March 11, 1898.

A bugle's call to attention interrupts a classroom of cadets at West Point—"Old Rosy" is dead! The announcement reverberates throughout the hallowed halls. General William Starke Rosecrans has died at his ranch in Redondo, California. A professor stops mid-sentence, closes his book, and removes the eyeglasses from the bridge of his nose. "To Rosy!" he calls, raising one arm, and a chorus to the General's passing is sent out by all. Everybody knew about "Old Rosy", West Point graduate, Civil War General, and U.S. Congressman from the State of California. By an odd set of circumstances he was almost President of the United States. Had Rosecrans been quicker to reply, he'd have been on the ticket with Abraham Lincoln.

[Courtesy of Marilee P. Meyer, Archivist-Research/Cullum files,
Association of Graduates, USMA, West Point, NY]

*Cadet Ernest Darius Scott, Cullum 3838,*
*United States Military Academy, Class Album, 1898, Pach Brothers*

Unaware of the implication Rosecrans' death will have in his life after graduation from the Point, Ernest D. Scott sits at the back of the classroom and whispers to his buddy about the upcoming traditional social events of June Week, and the long-awaited Graduation Dance. Ernest is a good-looking, fresh-faced cadet with sandy blonde hair and large blue eyes. With boyish gusto they recite: "To the ladies who come up in June, we'll bid a fond adieu; here's hoping they'll be married soon, and join the Army, too" (from West Point song, "Army Blue").

But for Ernest Scott and his fellow classmates, the traditional graduation and festivities will not be conducted. The United States has just declared war with Spain (April 1898), and young officers have been hurriedly called to duty. Many, including 2nd Lieutenant Scott, will be sent overseas to the Philippines. Therefore, delivery of the coveted diplomas by the Superintendent of the Academy, and a short address given by Professor Col. Peter Michie, take place on April 26 in the chapel, with little of the ceremony cadets come to expect. No big tent on the green lawn, no hop, no farewell dinner.

[Courtesy of Gallery Graphics]

*Off Duty.*

## THE PHILIPPINE INSURRECTION

In San Francisco, 2nd Lt. Ernest Scott and some of his classmates board the Naval gunboat USS *Bennington*. The ship is assisting the Army in transporting troops to the campaign in the Philippines. On board this vessel is recent Naval Academy graduate Ensign Tom Windsor. Tom is tall, strikingly handsome, dashing one might say, with dark hair and piercing brown eyes. Ernest and Tom meet for the first time aboard the ship and first impressions are less than favorable. Tom comes across arrogant, cocky, and boasts of his "girl back home" in San Diego. He also has a snide remark about the Army as the boys from West Point board the ship. And some of his shipmates chime in as well. Ernest is not thrilled with his first encounter with Tom, or the Navy. He hopes never to see either again and looks forward to disembarking on the island of Luzon.

However, fate has other plans. After his tour overseas, 2nd Lt. Scott is assigned to the Artillery District of San Diego, and arrives in that city in October 1901. The paths of these two men will cross once again, this time in San Diego, and the rivalry begins....

Alle begins to meet some of the other neighbors in base housing. Definitely a "joint operation," she thinks to herself when she learns of all the armed services represented up the street. There is a Coast Guard, and Marine family too, for example. (potential for character development)

Taking a break from unpacking, Alle clears a spot on the dining room table to set up her laptop. Her husband Scott checks in by email with news of the 710th in Afghanistan. She is grateful for the daily updates he sends her on the activities of the soldiers.

## FIRST SCENE IN AFGHANISTAN

The group from the 710th arrives in country. They "set up camp" and although the conditions are rough, their spirits run high. (not much military infrastructure in place yet during the early stages of the campaign). The dialogue between the youngest member in the unit "straight out the EOD schoolhouse" with the more senior members, will provide a rare glimpse into the well-trained and exclusive Army EOD community. By their conversation, the reader will learn about the tough curriculum required by the Army in this specialized and dangerous field.

The members of the 710th Ord Co ( EOD) are introduced and we begin to connect and "fall in love" with all of them and their unique personalities. Jake gets the reputation of being a renegade, Bill is the class clown, and Toby, the token rookie, etc. (character development)

The men and women of the 710th soon learn of their mission to accompany and assist the Special Forces "A" team in the search for Osama bin Laden and other perpetrators of 9/11 in the mountainous caves of Tora Bora. It is a civilian clothes operation and the job for the 710th is to destroy ordnance that would threaten the safety of the troops on the ground.

## NEXT SCENE TAKES PLACE BACK IN SAN DIEGO MILITARY QUARTERS AGAIN — PRESENT DAY

Alle goes grocery shopping at the Commissary at North Island Naval Air Station. The base is located over the bridge and across the bay from downtown San Diego, on the "island" of Coronado.

When she returns home from her outing, she notices Caroline's door is open next door, and stops in to say hello. Despite three rambunctious children under the age of four, and a husband on deployment, Caroline always has a smile on her face, a kind word for everyone, and a contagious carefree air about her. She has a wonderful sense of humor and she always makes Alle laugh. Their friendship grows as the weeks progress.

Once back in her own quarters, Alle heads for the front porch. The sun is setting over San Diego Bay and the remaining daylight streams through the large picture windows. She curls up in a pillow-cushioned wicker chair and once again delves into the writings and letters from the past. She is riveted...

## THE SAN DIEGO UNION.
### WEDNESDAY MORNING, DECEMBER 25, 1901.

# SOCIETY TURNS OUT
# AT FOOTBALL CONTEST

## ARMY TEAM WAS SUCCESSFUL IN SCORING OVER THE NAVY BOYS.

### The Only Six Points Made Were Within Four Minutes of the Close of the Game---Crowds Cheered Their Favorites.

SOCIETY TURNS OUT
AT FOOTBALL CONTEST

The society people and the friends of the army and navy succeeded in making a society event of the football game between the two arms of the service as represented by a team from the two companies at the barracks and a team from the training ship Alert. Possibly the two most notable features of the game outside of the playing, were the two carry-alls decorated, one with blue and gold, the colors of the navy, and the other with cardinal and blue, the colors of the army. [carry-all: a covered one-horse carriage with two seats]

The army party consisted of Leda Gerichten, now Mrs. Jerauld Ingle, Miss Elsa Wentscher, Miss Gerichten, Fred Ingle, and Captain Flemming, among numerous others.

The navy party is made up of Mrs. Gilmore of the Alert, Miss Susie May Wood and a Miss Elizabeth Wood, Mable Gassen, Miss Stella Klauber, Lena Sefton, and the goat, the mascot of the ship. They were supplied with the yells of the contending forces and they made them heard as they blew their horns and waved their blue and yellow or cardinal banners in the breeze...There was about an equal amount of noise from the two carry-alls, but at the end of the last half, when the army boys succeeded in scoring, the party in the cardinal coach had it their own way for the final score was 6 to 0 in their favor.

There were many other society people present at the game, the grandstand being well-filled and the sidelines crowded, but the crowds on the line were of the sailors and the soldiers.

There was some brilliant playing by army team members Lieutenants Masteller and Ryan. By a series of rushes, they crossed into navy territory and landed the ball for a touchdown well to the right of the goal post.

It was the first point of the game, and the crowd went wild. The army calls were heard on all parts of the field, and as the bugler sounded the assembly the entire personnel of the two companies gathered in the center of the field and made the echoes ring far out into the bay with their "Rah! rah! rah! USA. Sis, boom, Army!"

Toward the end of the game, the navy then kicked off once more, but the soldier who got the ball succeeded in bringing it back almost to the center before he was successfully tackled. And at that moment, the whistle sounded for the close of the game.

Once again we hear the words of a young Ella von Engel, "I remember meeting my beloved Ernest at an Army/Navy football game in San Diego on Christmas Day 1901. He was a recent West Point graduate and a newcomer to the Artillery District in San Diego."

On that Christmas morning, all of society turns out for a football contest held between two companies from the Army barracks, (the enclave of the Army before the construction of Fort Rosecrans) and a group from the visiting Navy ship USS *Bennington*. Much to Ernest Scott's dismay, he spots Tom Windsor, a lieutenant now, on the opposing team.

Tom is coaching another newcomer, on the Navy side of the house, Ensign Newman K. Perry, a graduate of the US Naval Academy, Class of 1901:

[USNA *Lucky Bag*, Class of 1901]

*Perry*

*Kneedler*

The Ingles, Gerichtens, Windsors, Larsons and other prominent families and civic leaders in the town are all in attendance. Mr. Larson is the President and owner of San Diego Bank and Trust in the heart of the city's growing financial district. It is at this event that we also meet the Army post surgeon Major William L. Kneedler and his wife, Lydia, for the first time.

Dr. Kneedler, as the locals called him, is a beloved physician living in a beautiful residence on Coronado. He grew up in the wealthy Chestnut Hill area of Philadelphia, and graduated from the prestigious University of Pennsylvania. After completion of medical school, William Kneedler entered the service and following the Spanish American War, was assigned as the personal physician to William Howard Taft who, of course, would later serve as the 27th President of the United States and Chief Justice of the Supreme Court.

Lieutenants Charles Ferris, John McBride, Lewis Ryan, and Kenneth Masteller of the 30th Coast Artillery Corps suit up for the Army team. Any military man not down in the dirt on the playing field, is rooting for his team from the sidelines. Now brevet Captain Ernest Scott, handsome and muscular, paces the yard lines with a raucous cheering and shouting, unaware of his admirers in the stands. For among the crowd applauding the Army boys, are Leda, Amy, and Ella, along with her best friend Elizabeth (nicknamed Lizzy), all with eyes for young military officers. Leda, the oldest, is quiet and reserved and always has her nose in a book. She is "handsome' or pleasant, as was said in that time. Ella is the beauty. She is stunning, tall, confident, and outgoing. Amy, the baby, is carefree, bubbly and adorable.

Lizzy and Ella have been "giggling girlfriends" since the age of two. Lizzy is a treasure and always up for a good adventure. She is lovable, 'a silly girl' and a bit clumsy at times; a follower as opposed to a leader. But most importantly, she is always a willing participant in Ella's many antics. They are kindred spirits and bosom buddies. The two could laugh for hours, over nothing at all. And get into more trouble.

It is a thrill for all the debutantes seated in the grandstand to gaze at athletic soldiers and sailors hiking the yard lines below. The girls are deliriously happy waving to the members of the 30th Coast Artillery Corps, hoping to steal their attention and affection.

The Navy party boasts its own cheering section, which includes Admiral and Mrs. Edward Windsor, the misses Sally Mae Wood, Lena Sefton, Stella Klauber, Mabel Stockton, and other daughters of high society and their aristocratic families. Almost as entertaining as the game, is the ship's mascot (a goat), and the carry-alls of the two teams: one decorated in blue and gold, the other, cardinal and blue. The elder members of the community comment on the humorous display of rivalry.

Game time is 2:30. The Army boys have the kick-off, and the ball lands among the sailors, who succeed in getting about 20 yards of the territory of the soldiers before they are held, not being able to force their way through the defense of the Army opponent. When the soldiers finally secure the ball, they are fortunate in getting in some fast plays, carrying the ball into the field of their opponents to the 10-yard line of the sailors. The whistle blows signaling half time; the score is 0-0.

Ella excuses herself for a moment, and slips through the crowd to get a closer look at one officer, whose name she does not yet know.

Ernest catches sight of her, but unfortunately at the same moment, Tom Windsor does too. Tom catches up to Ella and blocks her forward motion in Ernest's direction. Tom then kisses her cheek in playful adoration, and runs back onto the field.

Ernest glances back over his shoulder. Ella's stunning beauty has captivated his attention and he runs back to his teammates to inquire about her name and situation. Tom overhears his conversation and senses his keen interest. He blurts out, "That's Ella von Engel, she's my girl."

The Navy men kick off, and the soldiers, through magnificent team interference, carry the ball to the 30-yard line on the Navy side of the field. By a series of rushes and some brilliant playing by the Army team, they cross into Navy territory. Tom tackles Ernest with a vengeance, almost knocking the wind right out of him. Ernest falls to the ground. A time-out is called. On the next play, Army lands the ball for a touchdown. It's the first point of the game and the crowd goes wild, blowing horns and waving banners of both team colors. The Army calls are heard on all parts of the field, and as the bugle sounds, an assembly of the two companies gathers in the center of the field. Their echoes ring far out into the bay— "Rah! Rah! Rah! U.S. Army!"

When the whistle sounds to end the game, the score stands 6-0 in favor of the Army artillery. Young ladies, eager to meet team players, rush to the field, abandoning good sense and social expectation.

The next scene opens to the dry, sun-scorched, desert landscape in the Afghan countryside. The Soldiers of the 710th play an impromptu game of football, kicking up sand and passing the time, while awaiting official orders for their next maneuver.

The camaraderie within the 710th intensifies as the members of the unit travel by camel, donkey, and by foot to remote areas to investigate the caves in Tora Bora and clear them of explosives. Different personalities emerge as the inherent dangers of the mission escalate. Fear and excitement grow as the soldiers dismantle terrorist training camps and exploit intelligence for the CIA and DIA. They are some of the first soldiers in that hazardous part of the world during the early days of the war. At Tarnak Farms, Scott finds a piece of a wall destroyed in an earlier U.S. bombing raid. The wall contained a map, in front of which Osama Bin Laden once stood; it was captured on film in one of his infamous videos. Scott writes home to tell Alle about his unit's new acquisition.

She is thrilled to hear the excitement in her husband's email message that day. Yet at the same time, the news of his location makes it difficult not to worry for his safety. The feelings of uncertainty and vulnerability in 'the new world order' are still ripe; the pain and sorrow inflicted by the perpetrators of 9/11, still fresh in everyone's psyche. The country continues to walk on pins and needles and terror alert conditions are posted on the television for the very first time. People in the civilian world have the luxury of their loved ones close by, at home. But Alle doesn't. Her husband is in harm's way.

So Ella's words from the past always provide a timely escape for Alle from that harsh reality.

[Paul Holtz, Point Loma Camera, San Diego, California]

*Fort Rosecrans under Construction.*

## BACK IN TIME: THE BUILD-UP OF FORT ROSECRANS, CALIFORNIA

Southerly breezes blow and set sagebrush to wild dancing along the eastern shore and hillsides at Point Loma—an eight-mile peninsula jutting into the Pacific. Standing at the tip of the promontory, circling and surveying the panoramic view, Army Major Robert Henry Rolfe kicks at the dirt under his boot and notes the rugged landscape lain out before him. As Rolfe studies his surroundings, we hear his voice "Sir, I have the honor to report my arrival at this station, for duty in charge of the construction of public buildings at Fort Rosecrans, California." He is the Army Quartermaster sent by the War Department to begin the construction of the new post. It will house the members of the Artillery Corps assigned to protect the coastline and the entrance to San Diego Bay. The gun emplacements are already complete, the result of the Endicott Era construction.

Major Rolfe, sporting a distinguished mustache and tall and rugged with shoulders held high, is a bit overwhelmed at the daunting task that lies before him. During his years at Dartmouth College, Rolfe played on the first varsity football eleven and was the champion distance runner of his time. Yet no athletic arena seemed as forbidding as the uneven terrain on Point Loma. Building a complete military post from a site of sagebrush would be his greatest challenge to date.

He walks to the edge of the bay where contractors are just finishing the Quartermaster's Wharf. Supplies and equipment will be off-loaded at the site for the building of officers' quarters, two barracks buildings, the post hospital, stable, guardhouse and bakery.

From the wharf, Major Rolfe observes an approaching vessel. It is the government launch, General De Russy, which ties up at the dock. Aboard is Captain Ernest Scott who arrives to escort his new superior officer back to town, a short boat trip up the bay. With no buildings yet on the new Army post, Office of the Constructing Quartermaster is located downtown in the large, brick, Keating Building on Fifth Avenue. Off they go to the hub of the rising new city.

SACRED TRUST

[San Diego History Center]

*Keating Block (Building), Corner of 5<sup>th</sup> and F in Gaslamp Quarter*

The steamer docks at Santa Fe Wharf and the officers head up Fifth Avenue on foot, past popular Marston's Department Store, ornate bank buildings, and various quaint eating establishments. People who walk along the street nod at the two officers. When they arrive at the Keating Building, they bump into Ella von Engel just stepping out of her family's store, located right next door. She is dazed by her good fortune. Captain Scott introduces Miss Engel to Major Rolfe, and she is elated that the handsome officer knows her by name. Ernest is dashing in his uniform and she is charmed by his engaging smile.

About this time a rowdy gang comes frolicking up Fifth Avenue. Downtown, ships' crews are always eager to cut loose and traverse the worn trail to the redlight district known as the Stingaree, where saloons, gambling halls, and opium dens await them. Ladies of the evening call it home and whiskey runs through the veins of gentlemen callers. It's a blemish that taints the emerging upscale business district.

Embarrassed by the notion that the revelers have come from the direction of the Stingaree, Captain Scott puts his arm around Ella's waist and directs her away from the sidewalk. Ella catches her breath, stolen with the touch of Ernest Scott.

However, the encounter does not go unnoticed by Lieutenant Tom Windsor U.S.N., looking out the window of his father's jewelry store across the street. He evades their notice and ducks behind a curtain, the sting of rejection penetrating throughout his entire being. He feels threatened by this newcomer and plans his next move.

Outside, Mr. Jessop's street clock sounds the hour and Major Rolfe excuses himself to return to his office. He sits down at a large desk where a stack of letters and contractor bids awaits his attention. In the coming days and weeks, lumber, equipment, and companies of artillery soldiers will begin arriving at the new Army garrison.

*Coronado's version of Jessop's clock.*

*(Historical note: Jessop's Landmark Clock was actually built in 1907.)*

"You've got mail" – Alle finds a new message waiting for her from Scott:

Back in Afghanistan, a team from the New York City Fire Department has just delivered three pieces of the World Trade Center (WTC) to the troops. Coalition Forces, Special Forces, and Soldiers from the 710th are present when one piece is buried in Tora Bora in memory of the victims who perished three months earlier. A moving memorial service takes place at the site of the last battle with the Taliban. Everyone bows their head in prayer. It is a somber and emotional event that will remain etched in their memories forever.

*(This scene is based on an interview with SSG Ray Ertle from the 710th who was there with the Commanding Officer, CAPT Keith Nelson. Another piece of the WTC is buried in Kabul, the capital, and the last in Mazar-e-Sharif.)*

As the members of the 710th depart the memorial ceremony, one of the Special Forces (SF) guys pulls Scott aside. He insists he come over to meet another friend of his, named Mike, who is a Navy helo pilot, also from San Diego. As the men engage in small talk, Mike mentions he lives in quarters on the Naval Submarine Base. As the conversation progresses, they laugh when they realize they are neighbors.

They joke about the coincidence, and of course compare notes about their wives, Alle and Caroline, and recent similar emails from the homefront. The two men, like the women, hit it off right a way.

Scott and Mike's dialogue in Afghanistan will segue into a scene back at Officers' Row in San Diego. Alle and Caroline are sitting on the front steps catching up on the news of the day. Alle is having a bad day missing Scott. She is also sharing the most recent entry from Ella's journal since it relates to the construction of their homes and a budding new love story...

CAROLINE

Hey, just look at this place.

We got a million dollar view of the San Diego skyline, the Pacific Ocean, some fancy, schmancy, nuclear-powered submarines parked right outside our front yard, and a nice view of the Hotel del Coronado across the bay over there on Coronado.

So yeah, I can see why you're feeling a bit sorry for yourself.

Caroline is being sarcastic, trying to make Alle cheer up and laugh. It works.

CAROLINE (CONT'D)

We're living at the "Ritz" with an ocean view, courtesy of the US military. What's to complain about?

ALLE

But how do you deal with the loneliness?

CAROLINE

Gotta look on the bright side; you get the whole bed to yourself, and even better, the remote to the TV. Don't have to cook or clean if you don't feel like it for months on end. What other job lets you get away with that!

ALLE

(looking around at her new surroundings)

Yeah, who built these homes anyways? They're amazing.

CAROLINE

Dunno. Nobody does. Not so much as one book about the place. Went down there to the base library soon after moving in to ask around, but no one seemed to know.

[Courtesy of Johnny Martinez]

**BACK IN TIME**

FADE IN:

INT. EXECUTIVE MANSION FEB 1901 — DAY

The Commander-in-Chief, President William McKinley, and his Vice-President, Theodore Roosevelt, are gathered together in the Executive Office. The Vice-President is sitting in a chair, legs crossed, adjacent to the President's large and impressive mahogany desk. He is silent and serious, looking down, and taking notes.

Earlier that day, during a formal group assembly, Captain Robert Henry Rolfe, Quartermaster, USA was "commissioned into the Regular Army in person by the President with an expression of gratitude for his service in the Spanish American War." He has been summoned by the President to return to the same location, but this time, he comes alone and the meeting is held in private, behind closed doors.

PRESIDENT WILLIAM MCKINLEY
(with bravado)
Rolfe, my boy...Come in, sit down. Make yourself
comfortable.

PRESIDENT WILLIAM MCKINLEY (CONT'D)
(patting the young officer on the back and leading him to a seat )
...the Vice-President and I have heard great things about
you. Your distinguished brother-in-law and one of my
closest confidantes, General Brooke, has been singing your
praises for quite some time now. And from what he tells us,
you are to be commended for your hard work and efforts
during the last campaign in Cuba. And Vice-President
Roosevelt, better known to all of you in uniform as
Colonel Roosevelt of the Rough Riders, concurs.

The President reaches for a box of cigars on his desk. He flips open the lid
and leans slightly as he offers one to the young officer.

Well-done Son. We need more men, like you, to join the
ranks in our Army.

CAPTAIN ROBERT HENRY ROLFE
(clears his throat nervously while reaching for one of the cigars)
Thank you Sir.

PRESIDENT MCKINLEY
(puffs on his cigar)
Based on your military record and fine education as a
Dartmouth man, the Vice-President and I have a new
assignment for you. We think you are the right man for the
job.

The last war taught us that we need to take even greater
measures to protect our nation, and its coastlines.  Recent
events in history have shown us, that we can ill afford to
leave our harbors unprotected.

As it stands now, the troops manning the guns in San
Diego's Artillery District, are sleeping in tents and other
temporary quarters. They are in need of proper living
accommodations.  The military reservation on Point Loma,
named after our late and esteemed General Rosecrans,
needs a permanent garrison. So we are sending you to San
Diego to build them a post. The gun emplacements are
complete and target practice has begun. But the men of the
Coast Artillery Corps need a place to live. What do you
say, my boy? Are you up to the task, Captain Rolfe?

## CAPTAIN ROBERT HENRY ROLFE, QM, USA
I won't let you down Mr. President.

## PRESIDENT MCKINLEY
And rest assured young man, we are sending backup to assist you. Honorable Judge William Taft has recommended his former personal medical attendant, Major William Kneedler, for Post Surgeon.

And as for the Commanding Officer, we've selected an up-and-coming artillery officer. General Lawton spoke very highly of this young man and recommended him for brevet Captain based on his actions in the PI, before the General himself became one of the casualties of our nation's last conflict. His name is Captain Ernest D. Scott. He's a highly decorated war hero as well as distinguished graduate of the Point. (West Point)

## PRESIDENT MCKINLEY
(again patting Captain Rolfe on the back as he escorts the newly commissioned officer to the door)
So this is the team that the Vice-President and I have assembled.

Good luck, my boy. We expect to hear great things from you and your team in the months ahead.

## CAPTAIN ROBERT ROLFE
I won't let you down Mr. President.

*Exactly one hundred years later, at the same post of Fort Rosecrans, another President will ask the Soldiers stationed there (710th Ord Co EOD) to defend their homeland and our national security as well.*

*"Parallel stories of love, loss, and heroism."*

[Courtesy of Ann Rolfe Symroski and Patty Symroski, granddaughters of Colonel Rolfe]

*Rolfe*

Fort Rosecrans is taking shape. Hillsides are graded flat, basements are dug and lined with granite, and foundations of concrete are laid. Crude dirt roads bump along the building site. As the months roll along, Major Rolfe keeps tabs on construction, contractors, and costs, all the while making friends in high places. City leaders recognize and praise Rolfe's management of the building of the fort, and woo him socially. Major Rolfe is initiated into the prestigious Cuyamaca Club, a ceremony steeped in tradition.

Captain Scott, meanwhile, is secretly courting Ella von Engel. She is intelligent, well-bred and self-assured. But it is her physical beauty and zest for life that captivate him. Her pretty figure and beguiling smile attract him to her. She is mesmerizing and he is quite taken by her.

A chance rendezvous confirms their blossoming relationship...

Ella walks down the steps of her home towards the guest cottage in the backyard. A badminton shuttlecock (birdie) comes coasting down from above, landing by her feet. "Come join us, Ella!" yell Lizzy and her younger sister Amy, playing on the lawn. "We could use another player and your wonderful company!"

But the early California sun entices Ella to make her way to the family stables. It is the perfect day, she thinks to herself, to go riding on the heights of Point Loma.

### EXT. ELLA'S PARENT'S HOME/GARDENS — DAY

Lizzy is disappointed that Ella is not going to see Tom today when his ship pulls into port. Ella chooses the Army over the Navy.

LIZZY
(waving and shouting)
Do you want some company on your walk?

ELLA
Not today Lizzy. It's a beautiful day and I think I will go riding on Point Loma instead.

LIZZY
But Tom's ship is in port today, Ella. I thought you were going to meet him down on the waterfront this afternoon? If I had a man like that interested in me, I would never let him out of my sight for a minute!!

ELLA
(entering the family stables and looking back at Lizzy)
Tom will just have to understand this time.

*Shadows on the Sea The Cliffs at Pourville, 1882, Claude Monet, French, 1840-1926.*

EXT. THE CLIFFS OF POINT LOMA – AFTERNOON

Ernest follows Ella, riding horseback, up the slope behind Fort Rosecrans to the top of Point Loma. They spend some time galloping together, their laughter permeating the warm, fragrant air. They dismount, and walk hand-in-hand enjoying the panoramic and breathtaking view. It begins to rain. The wind blows Ella's large-brimmed Victorian hat from her head and loosens her hair. Ernest saves the day, retrieving her hat with his heavy boot and placing it back on her head, while stealing a kiss.

-------------------------------------------------------------

During target practice at Fort Rosecrans, Ernest captures a glimpse of Ella on her steed as she begins her ascent up the cliffs. He mounts his horse and catches up to her on the trail.
Ella looks over her shoulder and notices Ernest following her. She smiles, pleased to see him, and blushes. Her excitement grows as she watches him close the gap between them. The officer exudes a feeling of confidence as he finally catches up to her; the victor in the pursuit.

ELLA
Why Captain Scott, what brings you out here in the middle of the day?

ERNEST
Why, you do, of course, Miss Engel.

Slipping down from her saddle in her white linen dress, Ella can no longer pretend she doesn't have feelings for this man who has unexpectedly entered her life.

The attraction she feels for him, is undeniable now. His magnetism, allure, and military bearing are powerful forces that take hold of every fiber of her being.

### EXT. TIP OF POINT LOMA PENINSULA — AFTERNOON

Ernest takes the reins of both horses and ties them to a nearby tree.

Then he returns to Ella and as he approaches her, he gently reaches out for her hand. Feeling a bit timid by his bold public display of affection, she blushes again, but yet she doesn't let go.

He is so tall and handsome, Ella feels it necessary to divert her glance downwards for fear he may see her infatuation with him, reflected in her eyes.

She looks down again, hoping to avoid his notice of her stare.

Her pulse races by the touch of his hand in hers. The emotion is so powerful and exhilarating, she becomes light-headed and tips a bit; she is off-balance, no longer on solid ground with sure and steady footing.

Typically self-confident and unafraid, she is mad at herself for her nervousness and momentary lapse of self-assuredness in his presence.

This Army newcomer has ignited feelings in her that she never knew existed before. She quiets the inner turmoil just long enough to begin a conversation.

ELLA
Such a beautiful day I just couldn't resist the urge to take a ride and feel the wind and ocean mist on my face. It always clears my head and washes away my troubles.

ERNEST
And what could possibly give you cause for concern, being a girl of such considerate nature and impeccable standing in the community?

What could ever bring unrest to your kind, sweet heart?

Unable, of course, to reveal the truth behind her worries (her doubts about her love for Ensign Tom Windsor and guilt about her new feelings for Ernest) she manages to change the subject and divert Ernest's attention to the scenery. They walk hand-in-hand to a perfect clearing at the top of the cliff.

The panoramic view of the city from atop the Peninsula of Point Loma is breathtaking; the quiet, sleepy entrance to San Diego Bay on one side, the sparkling blue waters and rumbling roar of the mighty Pacific on the other, extending into infinity.

They watch below as the white-sailed ships dance in the orange afternoon glow. The view is stunning and is equal in magnitude to her attraction for this handsome young officer, standing beside her.

She is thankful when Ernest finally pulls her towards him and gives her a kiss. The emotion is intense, and raw passion erupts within her.

The effect of the kiss is terrifying and intoxicating at the same time. She struggles to keep her composure, for fear he can read her mind.

> ERNEST (CONT'D)
> Will I have the pleasure of seeing you outside your father's store again soon?

> ELLA
> (coyly)
> I'm not entirely sure Captain Scott. My social calendar is quite full as you can imagine.
>
> Major Kneedler, Captain Rolfe, and their wives are planning a picnic outing up here at the lighthouse to pick wildflowers. They are inviting some of the crews of the visiting naval ships as well as all your officers from the Army Barracks, so it should be a grand affair.

> ERNEST
> So will your beau, Lieutenant Windsor, be in attendance?

> ELLA
> And who says he is my beau, Captain Scott?

> ERNEST
> (excitedly)
> Why he does, of course! He calls you "his girl" and he broadcasts that fact and boasts about you to everyone!! Everyone and anyone who will listen...in the town, in the streets...and throughout the entire West Coast Fleet of the United States Navy for that matter!!

Ernest and Ella both begin to laugh.

Very relaxed now, Ella's subsequent movements are dream-like and surreal. Surprising Ernest, and herself, she lifts her hand and caresses his face softly.

Then she slides the back of her hand effortlessly down his strong cheekbones; almost as if to prove to herself that he is really real and not just a figment of her girlish imagination.

She runs her fingers through the loose strands of hair on his forehead and then, they kiss again. And it is magical.

Suddenly it starts to rain and the cool, wet, raindrops jolt Ella back into reality. Their lips separate.

                    ERNEST (CONT'D)
                      (teasingly)
          What's the matter?


                         ELLA
          (annoyed by the interruption of the rain)
          It never rains in San Diego!

Ella reveals her frustration and her annoyance, pouting like a young child who has just been refused candy.

Ernest notices the change in her demeanor, and tickles and teases her to make her laugh.

[Museo Sorolla, Madrid, Spain/ Giraudon/ The Bridgeman Art Library]

*Strolling along the Seashore, 1909 (oil on canvas) by Joaquin Sorolla y Bastida (1863-1923)*

And then a gust of wind picks up, releasing the ribbons of her hat and freeing her long brown hair.

The charming officer traps the Victorian straw sunbonnet with his heavy, leather, riding boot.

He chivalrously bends over to retrieve it, picks it up, and brushes it off gently...

ERNEST

Luckily for you Miss Engel...You have a hat.

As Ernest places it back on Ella's forehead to shelter her from the raindrops, he kisses her once again under its large brim. The couple lingers in the moment as the landscape begins to sparkle around them. They stand motionless, clinging to the romantic embrace, wishing it would never have to end.

The rain continues pouring down around them, but neither seems to care.

DISSOLVE TO:

The young lovers make a mad dash toward their horses, yelling their good-byes excitedly to one another as they climb back up into their saddles.

ERNEST (CONT'D)

I can't wait to have the pleasure of your company again Miss Engel! I am looking forward to the picnic. I will be there, even if it means gathering wildflowers with the United States Navy.

ELLA

I look forward to the occasion as well Captain Scott.

She smiles, understanding and knowing full well Ernest's underlying meaning and intentions.

Ella's heartbeat races, matching the speed of her horse's gallop down the winding trail and back to her family estate. Anxious to share the glorious details of this chance encounter, Ella jumps down from her horse, barely waiting for the animal to come to a complete stop. She bolts through the front door of the house, and yells out loudly for her older sister...

ELLA

Leda! Come quick! Where are you? I have something very important to tell you! Hurry!!

[Van Houten's Cacao]

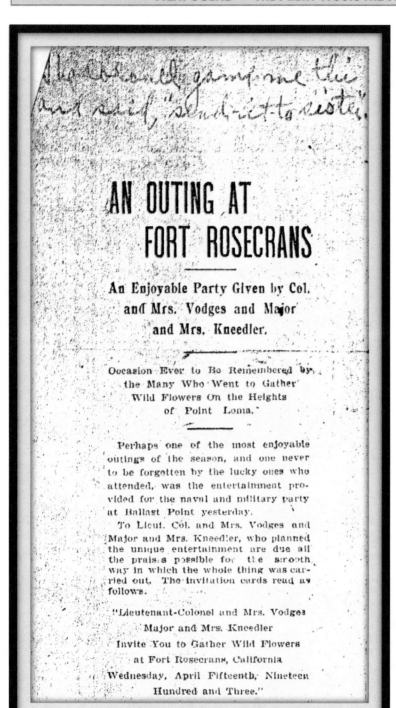

That spring a most unusual party to gather wildflowers on Point Loma is hosted by Major and Mrs. Rolfe and Major and Mrs. Kneedler. The invitation cards read as follows:

Major and Mrs. Rolfe
Major and Mrs. Kneedler
Invite You to Gather Wild Flowers
At Fort Rosecrans, California
Wednesday, April Fifteenth
Nineteen hundred and ....

*(Historical Note: Colonel and Mrs. Anthony Vodges and Major and Mrs. William Kneedler were the hosts of this delightful outing on April 15th, 1903.)*

LIEUTENANT-COLONEL AND MRS. VODGES

MAJOR AND MRS. KNEEDLER

INVITE YOU TO GATHER WILD FLOWERS

AT FORT ROSECRANS, CALIFORNIA

WEDNESDAY, APRIL FIFTEENTH, NINETEEN HUNDRED AND THREE

[Museum of Art, Rhode Island School of Design, Bequest of Isaac C. Bates, Photography by Erik Gould]

**Summer, 1909 (oil on canvas) by Frank W. Benson (1862-1951), American**

The first boat, the General De Russy, leaves the wharf downtown at 9:20 am and is accompanied by a barge filled with the elite of San Diego and Coronado. "Mule teams met the boats at Fort Rosecrans and all who so desired were driven up the beautiful winding cliff road to Point Loma lighthouse. Many walked and the sound of merry laughter was in order everywhere. Everyone agreed on one point, and that was that the bay, the city of San Diego, and the surrounding hills, were a sight never to be forgotten."

Ernest and Ella stroll along the trails with Major and Mrs. Rolfe. They look down upon Officer's Row and discuss its progress. The panoramic view from the top of Point Loma is drenched in spring pastel. Guests pick all the wild flowers they can carry. At 1:30 the bugle call gives notice that the picnic lunch is ready. People sit amidst the joyous occasion, and enjoy food prepared by Mrs. Rolfe and Mrs. Kneedler. The Engel sisters, their girlfriends, and all the young lieutenants in the 30th CAC stationed in San Diego agree to assist and see that every need is met. Officers from some of the visiting naval vessels in port also participate heartily in the festivities, including Ensign Perry and Lt. Tom Windsor from the USS *Bennington*.

Sitting on the same picnic blanket as Ella, Tom causes a stir with his presumptuous placing of a daisy in Ella's hair. Ella, none too pleased, removes the flower and gives it back to him. Witnessing the event out of the corner of his eye, Captain Scott comes to her aid in gentlemanly fashion. A jealous scene erupts between the two men. Some pushing ensues, but with their unsteady footing on the hillside, and in view of their senior officers, it doesn't last but a minute. Ella astutely places herself between them and makes light of the situation. Inside her heart is racing. She is thrilled and beaming over the fact that the two of them were fighting over her.

This encounter does not go unnoticed by Ella's mother, Mrs. von Engel, who looks on disapprovingly. Ernest knows that Ella's parents favor the popular Navy man Tom Windsor, with his influential family ties and future inheritance. Captain Scott will have to win them over.

[Joaquin Sorolla y Bastida, Spanish, 1863–1923, Museum of Fine Arts Boston]

*Lighthouse Walk at Biarritz, 1906*

As the deployment progresses, Alle and Caroline's friendship grows stronger. They always have fun sharing "war stories" about their spouses and gossiping about the Coast Guard family up "The Row."

Caroline invites Alle to her first official military wives' club meeting on Coronado. Alle already feels like an outsider as the token Army wife in Navy housing, so she is hesitant to attend, based on that fact alone. Never mind all the negative rumors and stereotypes that have been perpetuated and passed down for generations about these women.

Alle is obstinate, "I don't know Caroline, it's just not my thing. Don't make me go."

Caroline replies, "Oh come on. Don't be a scaredy cat, these girls are great, you'll see! They're tough as nails, and nice as can be, all rolled into one. Just remember one thing when you are there. The word NAVY stands for "Never Again Volunteer Yourself, so don't raise your hand for anything, and you'll do fine."

CAROLINE (CONT'D)

Look, I know there's a good chance you've heard us called the "knives club" and you've probably been told to "watch your back." But, in reality, the fact is ...no one else on the face of this earth knows better what you're going through right now, then me or one of them chickadees peeking out the windows next door. So don't be afraid to ask for help. They'll be there for you, you'll see. Believe it not, we're actually a family. Sure, sometimes you could call it a dysfunctional family, but, family none the less.

And put any ideas of rank out of your pretty little Army head. Once your husband leaves on deployment, it levels the playing field. No one's better than anyone else in this sorority. It's one for all and all for one at that point.

We're a team. Give it time, you'll see.

Stick with me, honey, and I'll show you the ropes and cover your back. I've been doing this for over 25 years now.

Yep, quarter of a century. Who knew?

Now they call me the COW. That's short for Commanding Officers' Wife, in case you didn't know.

Alle breaks a smile, albeit hesitantly.

"If they're anything like you Caroline, I guess I'll be Ok," says Alle and then grudgingly, "but just this once! I'll meet you out here in 10 minutes." Alle views the situation as an initiation or rite of passage. She tells herself she doesn't have to like it, she just has to show up, right?

Once she is there, she is pleasantly surprised to find that all the women are extremely friendly. They are a diverse group from all around the country; a cross-section of America which Alle finds very interesting. Far from the back-stabbing, finger-pointing group she feared earlier.

She comes away with the distinct feeling that these women take a lot of pride in their role as the spouses of military personnel. "We serve too" seems to be the motto for many of them living apart from their loved ones during a time of war. They sacrifice a lot for their country as well. Surprising to Alle, she can actually relate to them. She begins to see this club in a whole new light. When the service member is happy and quality of life for their families is good, active duty personnel are more likely to perform better at their jobs and remain in the military.

The work of military spouses goes beyond just "keeping the home fires burning" and "holding down the fort" behind-the-scenes. There's a strong correlation to military readiness and retention. Alle is beginning to view this group as an important secret weapon in national defense. Amazing!

Over the course of the deployment, Alle will come to appreciate the organization and what it represents. And she realizes that in time of need, these women are really the only ones who can truly understand how she is feeling, what she is going through, and how best to cope. There is a lifelong bond in the hearts of all these military spouses, which is unspoken and unbreakable. She begins to view her friends back in NYC very differently and her phone calls to them become less frequent as the movie progresses. (character transformation)

The members of the military spouses' club are also a very giving and generous bunch as evidenced in the number of charities they are involved with in the community. Another real eye opener for Alle.

On the agenda for that month's meeting was an announcement by the President of the Navy Spouses' Club who said the Coronado Public Library was looking for volunteers once a week to read to some of the retired military in the community. Many elderly members at the local Senior Center were no longer able to read on their own, due to failing eyesight and other physical ailments, and needed some assistance. Anyone interested in the program was to meet at the large gazebo at Spreckels Park across the street from the library. Inspired by the meeting, Alle decided to sign up, despite Caroline's earlier warning.

Rushing home and feeling upbeat about the day's events, Alle sends an email to Scott. However, on the other side of the world, his day was definitely not going as well as hers...

## NEWS FROM AFGHANISTAN

A detonation occurs which injures the Commanding Officer of the 710th, Captain Ken O'Neil. Walking along some tire tracks, there is a fuse under the ground, subsurface, covered up by sand. Captain O'Neil steps on it causing it to detonate. As a result, he is badly wounded. Scott carries Captain O'Neil's bloodied body out of the area on his back.

After initial medical treatment in Germany, the CO is sent back home to the United States to receive more care for his injuries which included the loss of some toes and scarring to his legs.

*(Historical Note: SSG Norm Willis (Ret) was out in the field with Captain Keith Nelson the day he was wounded. SSG Willis was the one who carried the CO out on his back that day. He told me that he kept Keith's dogtags in Afghanistan and said to Captain that he would hold onto them and hang them in the "breadhouse" until he came back for them in person. Despite his injuries, Captain Nelson insisted on returning to Afghanistan to bring home his unit, and the dogtags were waiting for him, as promised.)*

Alle always finds comfort in Ella's words and after hearing about the incident which wounded the CO, she is anxious to go back in time.

As she looks out the soft, white, billowy lace curtains blowing in her bedroom window, the blue sea outside creates a backdrop.

And off in the distance, she sees the majestic red-roofed turrets and ornate Victorian architecture of the Hotel del Coronado...

### EXT. SAN DIEGO BAY SHORELINE — MORNING

Ernest and Ella's second encounter is in a rowboat on San Diego Bay. The morning sunlight is glistening and the water is calm and tranquil.

Ernest is in uniform and Ella is in a traditional "Victorian" white shirtwaist and skirt, with hat and parasol. Ella steps into the wobbly boat adjacent to the dock.

ELLA
(giggling)
Are you sure this boat is seaworthy Ernest?

ERNEST
(reaching for her elbow to assist)
Of course. You don't trust me Miss von Engel?

ELLA
It's not that I don't trust you, but don't forget, you ARE
an Army man, NOT Navy.

Ella giggles again. And once out from under the watchful eye of her
attendant, Ernest leans into Ella, behind the shadows of her parasol, and
kisses her.

Local tuna fisherman, on their way out to sea for their morning catch,
wave, cajole, and offer cheers of good wishes for the couple.

Ensign Windsor however is seen peering at them from off in the distance
on the shoreline. His silhouette disappears among the multitude of fishing
vessels adjacent to the pier. His presence is an ominous reminder to Ernest
that Ella is "spoken for" and he will have to work hard to earn her
affections.

*Postcard, Fort Rosecrans, San Diego, California*

[Courtesy of Steve Ruhlen from the Colonel George Ruhlen Family Photo Collection]

*Officers Homes, Fort Rosecrans, California*

## BACK IN TIME

Houses stand like soldiers along Officers' Row and construction is nearly complete. Work presses on, but tonight, soldiers of San Diego Barracks and sweet young ladies from around the city attend a spectacular cotillion at the fashionable seaside resort, Hotel del Coronado. Officers from the visiting ship USS *Bennington* are also in attendance and include Ensign Perry and his bride, Vipont Doane, a debutante from Stockbridge, Massachusetts. It is obvious to all present, that the couple are deeply in love. While a student at the Naval Academy, Newman was given the nickname "Married Man," a lighthearted testament to his undying devotion for her.

The social occasion captures a picture of youthful innocence and sweet flirtation among coming-of-age girls attracted to good-looking and eligible officers in uniform. The gala is brisk and lively and the guests dance with the continual changing of partners in the magnificent Grand Ballroom. The scene resembles a fairy tale.

[Courtesy of American Antiquarian Society]

As if intoxicated, Ernest breaks away, stealing his partner Ella from the ballroom in a race towards the beach. The moon barely lights the sand under their feet. As they catch their breath, Ernest faces the ocean, clutching Ella's hand behind his back. The sea rolls in, then away again. Ernest turns and whispers, "Ella, the Army will take me places far away from San Diego. Yet I cannot bear the thought of living my life apart from you, not even for a day. I know it is selfish on my part to ask, but would you ever consider being my wife? It pains my heart to think of the sacrifices you will have to endure in the Army, leaving your close friends and family behind...All I have to offer you is my eternal love. Please accept my hand in marriage."

Ella hugs her soldier. "Of course, Ernest," she replies. "I have loved you from the first moment I saw you down on that silly old football field." She smiles and promises to love him always. "I am yours forever."

The couple stroll back to the ballroom, giddy with the secret exchanged between them. As midnight approaches, all of the guests gather on the beach outside to view the aerial salutes of a grand fireworks display: an electric shower of jewels and diamonds and prismatic whirlwinds illuminating the black sky. And under an umbrella of fire, Ernest pulls his fiancée close to him for a long kiss and an intimate embrace. Tom watches from afar and steams.

SACRED TRUST

Then all the young soldiers and lovely girls march off in a jovial line, making their way to the enclosed salt-water Plunge a short distance from the hotel. One after the other jumps into the pool, soaked, with not a care in the world.  Ella, no longer able to contain her happiness about Ernest's marriage proposal, whispers the news into Lizzy's ear, swearing her to secrecy. Lizzy is bursting with excitement! On her last jump, Lizzy being Lizzy, inadvertently blurts out the news at the top of her lungs, which echoes throughout the entire enclosure.

[San Diego History Center]

*Hot and Cold Saltwater Plunge, Tent City, Coronado, California*

Tom must thwart the impending union, or risk losing the love of his life forever.

**NEXT SCENE AT ELLA'S HOME**

## THE GARDEN SCENE

The following morning Ella wakes up and announces the news of her engagement to her parents, Mr. and Mrs. Charles P. von Engel. They are shocked by the revelation. Ella's mother can't imagine how she will explain the "disastrous situation" to her friends in the local ladies club, especially to her best friend Clara Windsor. The two women have sanctioned and promoted the match between Tom and Ella since their infancy.

## EXT. ENGEL ESTATE — MORNING

From the outside, the Engel home and grounds look like any other typical San Diego yard at the turn of the twentieth century, a large and inviting lot enclosed by the traditional white picket fence. However, once you pass through the floral-covered trellis gate and step inside, its boundaries are limitless. Mr. Engel, although a tough and keen businessman, is the keeper of the garden and takes great pride in his handiwork.

The gardens, gazebo, and fountain adjacent to their house and charming guest cottage, are enchanting. It is a place of exquisite beauty and quiet repose, transporting all unsuspecting visitors to a time and place resembling a fairy tale. Despite one's age, all "trespassers" become young again in mind, body, and soul; an exuberant feeling of pure delight.

Ella awakens the morning after Ernest's marriage proposal and decides to take a walk in the fresh morning air before approaching her parents with the news of her engagement. With Lizzy's innocent, yet untimely and unfortunate, announcement of it the night before in The Plunge (enclosed saltwater pool adjacent to the Hotel del Coronado), it won't take long in the small town for the news to circulate, and the secret to be revealed.

Ella jumps out of bed in her white, one-piece, bloomer-style sleeping attire and reaches for a sheer, floor-length wrap (wrapper) as she exits her bed chamber and heads for the backyard.

The aura of tranquility in the gardens is transforming and the color combination of overflowing nature takes her breath away.

She walks barefoot through the towering purple iris, vibrant pink hydrangeas, and bright orange California poppies, symbolically rising from the earth and dancing together in the early morning sunlight.

The "visual" musical symphony makes her heart full.

Ella is the Princess of the Garden, especially this particular morning. The splendor and warmth of this magical place surround and embrace her.

She makes her way to the pergola. Its canopy of green foliage shades the calm, still waters of the fish pond beneath. The bright orange creatures are mesmerizing below the surface as they glide languidly and gracefully under the lily pads and sparkling water, oblivious to the hustle and bustle, chaos and uncertainty, of everyday life and reality above them.

The young girl wanders through the dew-covered grasses. A small quaint, white footbridge lights a path over the deep dark waters of the pond, and the mysteries of life reflected within it.

A dark shadow emerges out of nowhere and startles her for a moment.

ELLA
Ernest, what are you doing here?

She turns her head left, right, and then behind her, hoping no one sees them. She closes the three, small, delicate buttons at the top of her nightwear.

ERNEST

I had to see you this morning Ella.

He reaches out and grabs her softly, and they kiss.

ERNEST (CONT'D)

I need to speak with your father right away and properly ask for his blessing and your hand in marriage.

ELLA

Ernest, you mustn't be here, please. I fear the news will reach them before you do, so I am on my way to tell them now.

ERNEST

Let me go with you.

ELLA

No, you can't go to my father looking this way. You never went home last night, did you? Your uniform is still damp and wrinkled from the Plunge. Please, you must leave here at once, before it's too late.

They part, the tight grip of their hands sliding to the tips of their fingers as they separate reluctantly. They both look back at each other, simultaneously, for one last glance, from off in the distance.

DISSOLVE TO:

Ella composes herself, and her words, to announce her engagement to her unsuspecting parents. She approaches the house and sees them through the rounded, glass, opaque windowpanes of the conservatory.

[Photographer Kurt A. Dolnier from Watertown, Connecticut, took the image of the Conservatory at the Lockwood-Matthews Mansion, Norwalk, Connecticut.]

## INT. CONSERVATORY WITHIN THE ENGEL HOME — MORNING

Potted plants and palms encircle Mr. and Mrs. von Engel, overflowing at the base of their feet. It is a beautiful and seamless blending of the outside with the interior.

Ella's father sits on one end of a white, ornate, wrought-iron bench for two. He is peering down through his bifocals at the morning newspaper, discussing the front page headlines with "Mother" sitting beside him with her needlepoint. It is their traditional morning ritual and with precision clockwork timing, the servants have placed the Engel Family silver-engraved coffee set adjacent to them on a small round table; a lace doily hanging down over the sides of the tiny, delicately stitched (embroidered) tablecloth.

MRS. FLORENCE VON ENGEL
Ella, my dear, please... Show some decorum and your good
upbringing.

MRS. FLORENCE VON ENGEL (CONT'D)
(sternly)
How many times must I tell you that a fine and proper
lady must always cover herself in the presence of others.

And... your Father is here Ella.

So do make yourself presentable to him, as well as in front
of the household staff.

MR. CHARLES P. VON ENGEL
Mrs. Engel, I have lived with four females in this household
for well over 20 years now. Nothing at this point could
ever surprise me about the wiles and whims of the fairer
sex.

Ella smiles, relieved to hear her father's humor, but hastily adheres to her
mother's wishes and closes her peignoir with its ribbon ties.

ELLA
Mother, Father, I have some news to share with you. I'm
glad you are both sitting down, but have no fear, it is of a
good nature. I have no doubt that you will be as elated as I
am, to learn of it.

At this point, Ella manages to secure their undivided attention. Her
mother removes her eyeglasses, now dangling from her neckline. She lifts
her embroidery stand, placing it off to the side, and stares directly at her
daughter now, with an unobstructed view.

Ella shares her news... Her mother erupts in disbelief and disapproval.

Florence, with utter disregard for her daughter's emotions, considers the news as a disgrace on the family and a blemish in her social standing. The unpardonable predicament is too much for the woman. She scolds Ella and accuses her of being thoughtless and ungrateful. "Your father and I have given you and your sisters everything: a beautiful home, expensive wardrobe, good education...And this is how you repay us? Oh, Ella, how could you do this to me?" Florence can't bear to face her circle of friends with the engagement announcement and braces for the unwanted gossip soon to follow.

Ella's devoted and loving father, on the other hand, is more understanding and sees strong character in this young Army man Ernest Scott. He gives Ella his blessing. This fact, of course, only incites Florence's anger even more.

Suddenly, there are three loud knocks at the door. It is a delivery boy with an envelope with Ella's name on it. When she opens the note, Ella notices a small gold locket enclosed as well. It is the most beautiful, delicate, and exquisite thing she has ever laid eyes on. **She opens the shimmering object. One half of the locket is engraved with the letter "T" and the other with the initial "E."**

EXT. ENGEL GARDENS — DAY

Ella returns to the gardens to contemplate the contents of the envelope. She once again welcomes the inspiring and soothing powers of that special place as she makes her final choice to begin a new journey and undertake one of the greatest challenges of her young life; the difficult decision to leave her beloved parents, sisters, home, and friends to marry into the Army.

Mr. Engel has created a place of rejuvenation and renewal on the grounds of his estate that will prove indispensable to him and his family during the upcoming months. Little did he know when he undertook the labor of love, that all too soon, the healing effects of that idyllic place would be a necessary prescription for one of his daughters in particular.

*Water Lilies by Claude Monet. Original in Musée Marmottan, Paris, France.*

SACRED TRUST

My dearest Ella,

I am completely devastated by the news revealed last night by Lizzy. I want you to be my wife. I have loved you since childhood. You and I were always meant to be together. Happily ever after, remember? I have decided to give up my career in the Navy for you. I will work at my father's store to support you. The business is growing and very successful. I'll be able to give you the world, Ella, and all the riches you desire. Do not leave me for that other man! He will never be able to provide the life of luxury you so deserve. He will never love you the way I do. When you come back to me, wearing the locket, I will have your answer.

I am anxiously awaiting your visit.

Forever yours,
Tom

**Tom never sees the locket again. It is the answer he dreaded.**

Alle meets Elizabeth Fairchild, the elderly woman from the Coronado Senior Center, for the first time at the park the following week. Alle likes her right away. She finds her regal in stature and demeanor. Judging by her clothing, a Lord & Taylor kind of gal. Very classy and well-spoken. She must have been stunning in her youth, thinks Alle, the lines in her face masking a perfect complexion.

Alle is so happy when she learns that Elizabeth was born and raised in New York too, so there is a common bond between them immediately. As the women get to know one another, Elizabeth opens up to Alle and tells her that she was orphaned as a child, at a very young age.

## FLASHBACK SCENE FOR ELIZABETH

One of her earliest memories was in a lawyer's office at the local county courthouse after her mother's funeral service. She remembers the large, suited man saying she was to remain with her grand-aunt until adulthood. The announcement was a devastating blow to Elizabeth. Her aunt was a nasty, old woman. Elizabeth never felt comfortable with her, loved, or wanted. She was a cold, stern, and distant figure. Elizabeth would never forget, or forgive her for, the way in which she brutally yanked her from her mother's arms and bedside, the day she passed away. It was such a thoughtless, callous, and cruel act towards a young girl, grieving the loss of her only parent.

She continues, "I remember kicking and screaming at that moment, and in an act of total defiance and desperation, I grabbed a small wooden box off my mother's nightstand, clutching it for dear life. I coveted the little "treasure chest," and I still do.

As the years went by, my grand-aunt sold off most of my mother's possessions. But, even to this day, when I open that small box and close my eyes, my mother and I are together again, holding hands, laughing, skipping, and whispering special secrets.

"So what brought you here to San Diego?" asks Alle.

**Elizabeth recounts the story of her mother's last words before her death. "Hero, San Diego." Elizabeth had spent most of her adult life trying to uncover the mystery of her father's identity.**

It became her lifelong passion and calling. When she turned of legal age, she immediately packed her belongings, left her grand-aunt and never looked back. She headed straight for San Diego, obsessed with learning the truth about the father she never knew. Her search led her to Coronado. To Elizabeth, like so many people, it was an island paradise. She fell in love with the quaint little town and was content to spend her life and the rest of her days on the "Crown Jewel" of Coronado, California.

Alle was anxious to hear more, but a cool breeze blew in off the ocean. Elizabeth developed a slight chill and so their enjoyable afternoon gathering and tea party beneath the gazebo, would have to come to a close. But Alle promised to return and they would continue her story the next time they met.

*Gazebo at Spreckels Park on Coronado.*

### ALLE'S BACK HOME IN MILITARY QUARTERS ON BASE

"Hi Alle! How did things go on Coronado with the Senior Citizens?" yells Caroline from the adjacent upstairs bedroom.

Alle replies, "Actually, I met the most delightful woman. She is from New York too, so we connected right away. I told her about the letters I had found and she sounded extremely interested in hearing more about them. I promised to bring them and read them aloud next time we meet. She's loves history too. She's been doing research on her family genealogy for years."

Caroline responds, "That's great news, Alle. I'm so glad things worked out. I'm sorry I can't talk more right now, but I have to run and wipe a nose, change a dirty diaper, fix a toilet, change a lightbulb, a flat tire or something... Gotta love deployments! Say hi to Scott for me in your next email!"

"I will!" Alle is anxious to write to Scott and tell him all about her new acquaintance at the park.

Dear Scott,

First, before I forget ...Caroline says hello. She is so amazing! I admire her more every day. I don't know how she raises those three kids alone. Keeping up with the household chores, the homework, shopping and cleaning, ...I have to give it to these military spouses, they are a tough bunch! And yet they always make it look so easy!

Anyway, did I tell you I am reading to an elderly woman on Coronado once a week? Her name is Elizabeth Fairchild. She is wonderful! I'll share more about her in the days to come.

Leaving the best for last....Happy Anniversary Soldier!! You didn't forget, did you? One year ago today, but it feels like a lifetime ago. I miss you, especially today. Wish we could be together. We'll celebrate when you get home.

Love always, hugs and kisses,
Alle

(The audience feels the emotion and understands how hard it is for our troops and their families to spend holidays, birthdays, and anniversaries apart.)

Coincidentally, on the same date as Alle's anniversary, we will hear Ella describing her wedding to Captain Ernest D. Scott:

It didn't take long for Mrs. Florence von Engel's friends to convince her that having a son-in-law who is an officer from the USMA (West Point) instead of the USNA (Naval Academy), would never be considered a demerit in her social standing in any way. Her swift change of heart is almost comical. Upon hearing the approval from the female "powers that be," Florence quickly reverses her position on the matter. She makes peace with her daughter's decision and then reconciles with her very understanding, and long-time friend, Clara Windsor. Florence's attentions quickly shift to planning the wedding and making it the social event of the year.

The most influential couple in San Diego, Mr. and Mrs. Heber Ingle, have announced the wedding of Captain Ernest Scott of the Coast Artillery to Miss Ella von Engel, and consent to be the witnesses on the marriage certificate. Society is abuzz.

Sun shines brightly over San Diego in the afternoon of October 8th, 1903. St. Paul's Episcopal Church, on the corner of 8th and C, is filled to the outer doors with family and friends of the popular couple. There is much excitement in the town regarding this union between the local daughter of high society to one of the brightest young artillery officers in the Army. "An army wedding is always a popular society event. Even away from the military surroundings of an army post, the uniforms of the participants and the strict attention to detail add a charm that is wanting in a wedding in civil life. Then too, there is a touch of romance about a girl casting her lot with the army..."

There's even a double line of onlookers standing outside, hoping to catch a glimpse of the bridal party. Including one unexpected guest - Lieutenant Tom Windsor. There is a hush in the church as he enters the sacred hall. It is Tom's last hope that Ella will change her mind and not show up at the church.

Yet, his dream is quickly shattered as the large double doors open, and Ella walks in.

She is a stunning vision in her white satin bridal gown, bodice of rare Venetian point lace, and long tulle veil falling to the edge of the court train. The fabric in the dress is embroidered with pearls and beads, and she sparkles as the light shines in from behind her.

But for Tom, the pain is more than he can bear and he immediately exits out a side door, visibly devastated and distraught.

The choir enters and moves to the altar area. The church rector is a close family friend, Reverend Charles L. Barnes. He steps forward from the side aisle to face the groom and his groomsmen. Ernest, his best man, and the ushers wear the full dress uniform of their respective rank and branch of service. They line up at the chancel area, which is draped with an American and a Regimental flag, giving the occasion a distinctly military character.

The cathedral is beautifully decorated. The prevailing colors are "scarlet and gold" out of compliment to the artillery branch to which the groom belongs. The floral decorations are large and artistic. The end of each pew is draped with a white tulle ribbon secured with delicate crimson and yellow roses. And rays of sunlight illuminate the stained glass windows, creating a spectacular prism effect throughout the entire church.

As the bridal party congregate in the back, Ella's younger sister Amy, breaks away from the group, rushing to her big sister for one last hug. "I don't want you to leave me," she cries in anguish. Ella looks at her adoringly, "Don't worry my dear, sweet Amy. You will come visit us often. Promise me that you will? " "Of course I will Ella," Amy answers with happiness and renewed excitement in her voice.

To the strains of Lohengrin's "Wedding March," the bride and her party walk from the rear of the church, past guests that nearly block the center aisle. "Two dainty little maids," Ella's young cousins, lead the procession wearing white dresses with puffy sleeves and blue sashes. In their hair are crisp, oversized, matching blue bows that sit like crowns atop their heads. They look angelic as they gently drop rose petals from their baskets to guide the wedding party down the aisle.

The bridesmaids Amy von Engel, Lizzy Larson, Elsa Wentscher, Stella Klauber, Sally Mae Wood, Mabel Stockton, and Mattie Livermore come next. All the young ladies are becomingly gowned in white silk with blue satin sashes. The only ornament that is worn by them and the maid of honor is a small pin with crossed artillery guns of gold, set in rubies and diamonds. These are gifts from the bride. They carry baskets with blue ribbons and white cosmos flowers.

Ella's sister Leda, the maid of honor, appears next. She is dressed in an imported creation of light blue crepe de Chine. It is a superb gown, befitting her role. She carries a bouquet of miniature rosebuds.

And then the bride herself, so elegantly dressed, escorted on the arm of her distinguished father, Charles P. von Engel.

Ella turns her gaze to her handsome husband-to-be, nervous about assuming her new role as the wife of an Army officer. She is aware that she is entering a world of "spit and polish" very different from her pampered upbringing. However, her deep love for the military man dissolves any pangs of uncertainty.

Ernest walks his bride to the altar, and the full Episcopal ring service is officiated by Rev. Barnes. At the close of the impressive ceremony, the bridal party leaves the church to the triumphal sounds of Mendelssohn's "Wedding March." An arch of swords is made by the groomsmen and the bride and groom pass under the sabers. Ella, you're in the Army now!

Late into the night, hundreds of guests weave in and out of the wedding reception at the Engel estate at 1834 C Street. The house is festive and in the living room, the American and German flags hang over the mantel. Even the lawn is elaborately festooned with white lights throughout the lush gardens and trees.

An elegant supper is served and a full orchestra plays during the entire evening. The customary songs of "Army Blue" and "Benny Havens" are repeatedly called for; "their inspiring notes carrying every officer back to his cadet days at West Point." The traditional Service Punch, always a remembered part of any Army wedding, was served during the toast. The wine punch had been specially ordered, bottled, and shipped from Delmonico's in New York City for the occasion.

The dancing is endless and continues well into the evening "until it is necessary for the bride and groom to run to catch that bete' noire—the last car."

[San Diego Union, October 9, 1903]

*56 Beaver Street, New York, N.Y.*

*(Historical Note: Newspaper articles of the actual wedding of Capt. Ernest Scott to Ella von Gerichten in San Diego in October 1903, the wedding of Ensign Newman Perry to Vipont Doane the exact same weekend in Stockbridge, Massachusetts, and the magnificent wedding of Major Kneedler's daughter on Coronado in April 1909 can be found in* Kneedler *book. I incorporated elements from all three into the wedding scene here.)*

At midnight, the parents of the bride and the wedding party escort the couple several blocks to the Santa Fe train depot. Ella must say goodbye to her mother and father for the first time in her life. Steam hisses from the dark locomotive as Ella and Ernest board the railway car to begin their wedding trip and journey to their new home with the 80th Coast Artillery Corps at Fort Schuyler, New York. They leave a trail of teary eyes and waving handkerchiefs alongside the disappearing train tracks.

[Photo in public domain via Wikipedia]

*Santa Fe Train Depot.*

Some of the young people continue the celebration downtown. It is there that Tom meets up with the partygoers. He appears extremely depressed, downtrodden, and disheveled. **Lizzy steps forward to console him. They talk long into the night, and in a moment of passion, their actions will change the course of their lives forever. Lizzy becomes pregnant.**

Alle wipes away tears after reading about the heart-breaking farewell taking place at the train station. She recalls her own military wedding with the arch of swords at the chapel at West Point and misses Scott even more.

*Chapel at West Point*
*After shooting this photo of the chapel, I witnessed the wedding ceremony taking place inside.*

A week later and to cheer herself up, she decides to call Elizabeth to see if she is up for another reading session. "It's a beautiful southern California day and getting out of the house and driving towards the beach will do me good," she tells her friend. She continues, "Scott and I were apart on our first anniversary last week, so I'm feeling a bit sorry for myself. I miss him, and my family back in New York, so I just don't feel like spending the day alone. Are you up for a visit?"

"Of course," says Elizabeth. "Come... please come, I'll be waiting for you in the usual spot. "

Alle is also very anxious to share the letters about Ella's wedding with Elizabeth.

"Ok, Elizabeth, I have monopolized the conversation for hours now," says Alle as she looks up from the pages of Ella's notebook. "It is your turn. Tell me more about your search for your father."

Elizabeth starts, "Shortly before I arrived in San Diego, there was a terrible fire at the County Administration Building. Unfortunately for me, the timing of its occurrence, as well as the destruction it caused, proved catastrophic. All the files, documents, and "vital records" that may have shed some light on my paternal lineage were completely destroyed. All hope was lost. My hope was lost. I had come so far and I was so close. Yet, in the end, everything went up in smoke. Life is not always easy, is it Alle?"

That evening, Alle is shocked to learn that very soon after her wedding, Ella returns home to San Diego, alone. She is homesick. She misses her mother, father, Leda, Amy, and her close-knit circle of friends, especially Lizzy. She realizes that she never fully appreciated the idyllic life she lead in San Diego, until she was forced to leave it all behind.

Life on an Army post is very different, even difficult. Sounds of reveille at daybreak, booming guns during target practice, and daily drills, parades, and inspections outside her front door. Sparse government-issued furnishings and post regulations. A reputation to keep. The strict military protocol is foreign to Ella and different from her pampered upbringing.

During her visit back home with her parents, Ella "uses her influence" and contacts the Secretary of War to have her husband transferred back to the Pacific Coast. Captain Scott received the cheerful news in an order from Washington.

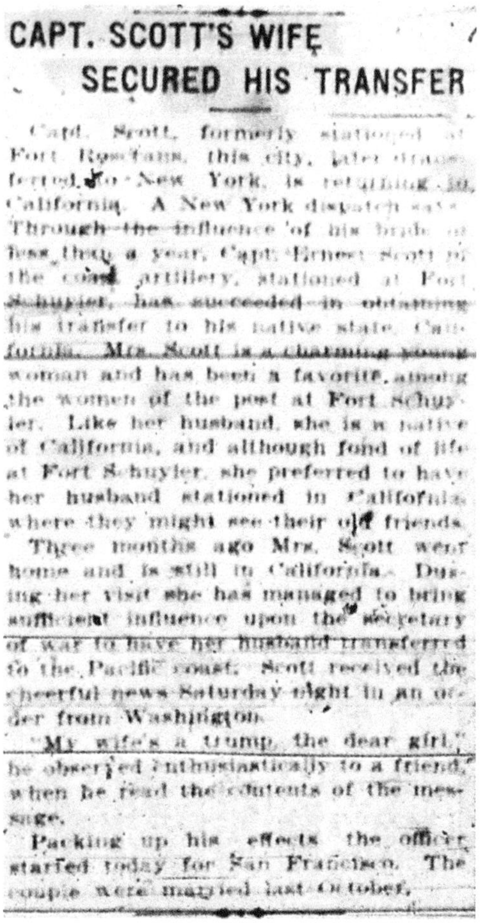

CAPT. SCOTT'S WIFE SECURED HIS TRANSFER

Capt. Scott, formerly stationed at Fort Rosecrans, this city, later transferred to New York, is returning to California. A New York dispatch says: Through the influence of his bride of less than a year, Capt. Ernest Scott of the coast artillery, stationed at Fort Schuyler, has succeeded in obtaining his transfer to his native state, California. Mrs. Scott is a charming young woman and has been a favorite among the women of the post at Fort Schuyler. Like her husband, she is a native of California, and although fond of life at Fort Schuyler, she preferred to have her husband stationed in California where they might see their old friends.

Three months ago Mrs. Scott went home and is still in California. During her visit she has managed to bring sufficient influence upon the secretary of war to have her husband transferred to the Pacific coast. Scott received the cheerful news Saturday night in an order from Washington.

"My wife's a trump, the dear girl," he observed enthusiastically to a friend, when he read the contents of the message.

Packing up his effects the officer started today for San Francisco. The couple were married last October.

*[San Diego Union,*
Friday morning, August 5, 1904]

"A New York dispatch says that through the influence of his bride of less than a year, Capt. Scott of the Coast Artillery, stationed at Fort Schuyler, has succeeded in obtaining his transfer to California.

"Mrs. Scott is a charming young woman and has been a favorite among the women of the post...and although fond of life at Fort Schuyler, she preferred to have her husband stationed in California where they might see their old friends."

ERNEST
(reading the contents of the message)

My wife's a trump, the dear girl.

Ella is well aware of the fact that she may once again have to come face-to-face with the man she jilted, Tom Windsor. There are a number of social events which could force their unintended reunion. It is a risk she is willing to take.

*(Historical Note: Major Rolfe hosted the Grand Opening of Fort Rosecrans on June 16th, 1904. Prominent citizens from around the city came to inspect the work and celebrate its completion.)*

Businessmen, politicians, and members of the Cuyamaca Club attend the anticipated opening of the new buildings at Fort Rosecrans. They gather on the porch of the commandant's residence, overlooking the entrance to San Diego Bay. Constructing Quartermaster Major Rolfe offers a few words of welcome.

A tour along Officers' Row follows and everyone agrees that the buildings are "firm and well-built in every particular". The magnificent homes impress the honored guests. As they inspect the double lieutenants' and the double captains' quarters, they comment favorably on the structures, which include wrap-around front porches, ornate pressed-tin ceilings, "secret" staircases, built-in china cabinets, and other striking architectural features.

Refreshments are served at the guardhouse by the steward of The Cuyamaca Club. Mayor Frary raises a toast to Major Rolfe for his distinctive efforts at Fort Rosecrans and awards him the invitation and honor to be Grand Marshal of the city's upcoming 4th of July celebration. Major Rolfe accepts and then makes the announcement that Captain Scott has just received official orders back to San Diego and assigned the position of first Post Commander of Fort Rosecrans.

## 4TH OF JULY

Firecrackers explode to announce the dawn of Independence Day.
It is an era of commercial revival in the city and each local business occupies a carriage in the highly anticipated annual parade. Ten automobiles decorated with the utmost taste and with all the flowers of the southern land begin the procession.

The seats are decked with beautifully gowned ladies, including Mrs. Ella Scott, her sisters Leda and Amy Engel, Lizzy, and all of the daughters of San Diego's gilded age.

Next, the 1$^{st}$ division guard, lead by the police chief and his staff, followed by Grand Marshal Rolfe, looking every inch the soldier trotting along on a superb charger. The military is greeted with applause as they march along the parade route. Mexican War Veterans in carriages come next, followed by the Guard of the Army Regulars. The parade moves on with Foreign Consuls and Army and Navy officers in carriages. Behind them, are elaborately decorated bicycles, one after another.

After the parade, everyone enjoys a day bursting with activities—rousing music by the City Guard Band, speeches, singing, reading of the Declaration of Independence, swimming competitions, and yacht races.

By nightfall, the scene is the most elaborate ever attempted in San Diego—the electric lighting of Coronado and the shores of Glorietta Bay; a parade of fifty powerboats wildly decorated by theme and outfitted with thousands of Chinese lanterns.

## PRESENT TIME

Alle has the TV on, and in the background she hears a broadcast alert on the "Fox News Channel." "Airport authorities have arrested a man, believed to be a terrorist, carrying a bomb in his shoe......"

## AFGHANISTAN

Scott and some of the other members of the 710$^{th}$ Ord Co (EOD) find evidence needed to connect the infamous "Shoe Bomber," Richard Reid, to Al Qaeda.

*(Historical Note: SFC Antony Hammerquist and SSG Norman Willis (Ret) describe the events that led to the discovery of evidence which resulted in the subsequent indictment and conviction of Richard C. Reid. It will be a behind-the-scenes look at the role that the Soldiers of the 710$^{th}$ Ord Co (EOD) played in bringing this terrorist to justice. Anyone who has ever had to remove his or her shoes at a security gate at an airport will relate to this scene in the film.)*

Alle and Caroline are out for a walk in the neighborhood. They pass a large Mayflower Van Lines truck outside the home of the Marine family.

Caroline stops and says to one of the workers, "Please don't take this personally sir, but you are sort of like the Grim Reaper in these parts. Don't come for me next!" The man understands and laughs. Caroline continues, "We just get a little nervous around here when we see cardboard boxes everywhere."

## MOVING DAY — BACK IN TIME — OFFICERS ROW

The town is abuzz with the news of Captain Scott's return to the city and his impending arrival. His reunion with Ella is warm and loving. They have missed each other immensely during their extended separation. Captain E. D. Scott reports for duty as the first Post Commander at the new Fort Rosecrans in August. As was typically done during the early years of mounted troops, the "newlyweds" were greeted by personnel at the post, riding out on horseback to escort the couple into the garrison. A reception was held on the spot. So too, the tradition begins at Fort Rosecrans.

[Courtesy of the Pennsylvania Academy of the Fine Arts, Philadelphia. Joseph E. Temple Fund]

*The Crimson Rambler, Philip Leslie Hale, ca. 1908, Oil on canvas, unframed, Acc. No. 1909.12*

Major Rolfe, Major Kneedler, members of the Coast Artillery Corps and their families, hurry out to meet Captain and Mrs. Scott. Officers and enlisted personnel stand for the formal introduction of the couple. A salute is then rendered. Two soldiers present them with a silver bowl bearing the regimental crest of the 115th Coast Artillery. It will become a most treasured gift with deep sentimental attachment. As the regimental band plays, the men and their wives whisk the couple to their assigned quarters on Officers' Row. Ernest carries Ella over the threshold, kissing her as he crosses. She is home. Home in her beloved town of San Diego with her husband. Her happiness at that moment is boundless!

### INT. ELLA AND ERNEST'S HOME — EVENING

Captain Ernest D. Scott is the new Commander of the 115th Coast Artillery Corps. He has just returned home for the evening after his first day on the job at the new Army headquarters building at Fort Rosecrans. He is tired and looks a bit disheveled following his many long and busy hours in the office. After kissing his wife warmly and tenderly, he is content and leaves the room while Ella continues scurrying about the kitchen. She welcomes him home, asks hurriedly about how his day went, but she seems preoccupied and goes about her business and kitchen duties, oblivious to his condition of fatigue.

> ELLA
> (Smiling to herself, aware of her own silly exaggerated high drama.)
> Ernest, I've already started planning the menu for our first official party.
>
> I can't even begin to tell you how excited I am at the thought of cooking New Year's day dinner here at our new home. I swear we must be the luckiest couple in the entire US Army!! We will be the first to host this annual Army tradition at Fort Rosecrans! It will be historic!
>
> Now I simply must get back to work. This is my first official social event as the new Commanding Officers' wife, and I want everything to be perfect. Just perfect. This meal has to be one that our friends, and the entire US Army, will be talking about for years to come.

> ERNEST
> I'm sure everything will turn out just fine, my darling. You have nothing to worry about. They will love you, and your cooking, as much as I do.

ELLA

What do you think about us serving duck?  Or maybe a
roast? I must call "Mummy" at once and see what she says.


When Ella doesn't get an immediate response from her husband, she
turns around, hears a muffled sound from the adjacent room, and yells
out to him, a bit annoyed.


ELLA (CONT'D)

Ernest, Ernest, where are you?


Ella stops her slicing of vegetables on the butcher block countertop,
wipes her hands on her apron, and goes into the parlor. She finds Ernest
fast asleep on the couch. He has practically collapsed in a state of
complete exhaustion after his first day on the job as the new Post
Commander.


Ella goes over and smiles. She kisses him gently on the forehead, loosens
the tight collar of is uniform, and removes the heavy, dusty, boots from
his feet.

# WOMAN GRANTED PILOT'S LICENSE
# WINS HONOR THROUGH PROWESS

## Mrs. Celia A. Sweet Qualifies To Navigate Large Power Craft on Bay.

Mrs. Celia A. Sweet, First San Diego Woman to Be Granted Pilot's License for Bay, and One of Fast Boats (The Relue) Which She Has Driven.

For the first time in the history of its bay, San Diego has a woman pilot. Last week a license was issued from the San Francisco hull inspector's office to Celia A. Sweet "to operate or navigate a craft of not more than sixty-five feet in length, propelled by machinery, in whole or in part by gas, gasoline, petroleum, naptha or electricity, and carrying passengers for hire."

The license is dated June 29, 1912, and is signed by James Guthrie and Joseph P. Dolan, United States inspectors of hulls.

Mrs. Sweet is the wife of Jim Sweet, a member of the firm of Winston & Sweet, boat builders. Of the flotilla of bay craft Sweet has designed and built perhaps the Lady Meredith, The Jester and Relue are the best known.

For a number of years Mrs. Sweet accompanied her husband on his trips about the bay lighting the beasons when he had that contract, and it was this practice that fitted her to win trophies and a bay license. Two years go, in her husband's speedy Relue, Mrs. Sweet won a handsome cup offered by the Tent City management, and the same season, in a series of races sponsored by the San Diego Yacht club, she showed her ability to pilot in the racing game by defeating the best helmsmen in the harbor and winning a cup offered by the club. A number of times Mrs. Sweet has taken her women friends "outside" for a day on the ocean, and in other ways has shown herself a genuine navigator. There are pilots and then some more pilots on the bay, but Mrs. Celia A. Sweet is San Diego's first and only woman pilot.

*In 1912, Celia Sweet will go down in history as San Diego's first female, federally-licensed, harbor boat pilot. She is a woman ahead of her time, a pioneer and trailblazer in the boating world.*

[*San Diego Union*, July 3, 1912]

*Postcard, Cobblestone Point, Ballast Point Lighthouse, entrance to San Diego Bay, California, with Fort Rosecrans in the background.*

CUT TO:

DISSOLVE TO:

The morning after her move into quarters at Fort Rosecrans, Ella takes a walk to explore her new surroundings. She meets young Celia Sweet who is out for her morning swim, and sunbathing at the water's edge. Ella is happy to learn that Celia is married to the lighthouse keeper at the Ballast Point Lighthouse, on Cobblestone Point.

Celia's house, with its attached tower and beacon of light, is within walking distance and view of Ella's quarters. The lighthouse structure is storybook beautiful. There is a mystical and magical feeling about the location that both intrigues and frightens Ella; its setting is romantic and treacherous at the same time. The beam of light emitted from the lighthouse lens can be seen in the distance from Ella's parlor window. It creates a ghost-like vision in the early morning mist and then transforms into a nautical navigational tool in the dark of night.

The two young neighbors soon become friends. Ella enjoys spending time at the lighthouse and away from some of the mundane domestic duties at home.

And Celia is delightful: a wonderful mix of warmth, charm, and humor. Ella admires her bright, young friend. Celia possesses both an inner, and outer, strength that is refreshing to Ella, especially in the male-dominated society of the day. Celia is a woman ahead of her time, a pioneer and trailblazer in the boating world.

CUT TO:

INT. MASTER BEDROOM — OFFICERS' ROW — MORNING
Not long after their move into quarters, Ernest tells Ella he must leave for D.C. for a short time on urgent business. He must depart for the east coast immediately. Ella is left alone to set up their new home. She complains as she looks about the bedroom of her new home which is filled to the brim with massive boxes, wooden cartons reaching to the rafters, and floors littered with traveling trunks.

> ELLA
> But Ernest, how could you! How can you leave me like
> this? Just look at this place, it's a mess. Boxes everywhere.
> What if one of the other couples comes to call this evening.
> Why I can hardly see a path to my dressing room.

> ERNEST
> I'm sorry my dear, but duty calls. I can't ignore a telegraph
> from Washington. It must be an urgent matter. Take your
> time unpacking. Plenty of time for evening calls later on.

Ernest brushes aside one of the panels of the lace curtains and soaks up the view outside.

Looking below, he sees an Army striker making his way up the steps towards the front door.

A female servant knocks on the door of the bedroom, announcing the soldier's arrival and his request to escort Captain Scott to the station. The train will be departing shortly.

> ERNEST (CONT'D)
> Enjoy our new home and surroundings Ella, for both of us.
> Go for a swim or take a walk on the beach. It's beautiful
> outside. I'll be back before you know it.

Captain Scott ensures the proper closure of all the brass buttons adorning his coat, reaches for his hat, and kisses his wife goodbye.
Watching Ernest hesitate for a moment in front of the mahogany mirror to check his uniform one last time, Ella suddenly remembers her new role as Commanding Officer's wife. Knowing the importance of punctuality in the Army, she does a quick "about face" and practically pushes him out the door.

SACRED TRUST

As Captain Scott rides off into town, Ella swings open the upstairs window and waves proudly to her husband until he is no longer in sight. Taking her husband's advice, and using any excuse to avoid unpacking, Ella heads towards the sea for an afternoon walk. She makes her way towards the lighthouse in the distance.

Strolling in front of the quarters down Officers' Row, Ella sees a new Army wife, visibly "with child," moving in next door.

The woman is carrying an oversized lamp up the front steps. Ella stops to offer assistance, "Here let me help you, you shouldn't be carrying that in your condition" and meets newcomer Mrs. Jean Vincenheller Dengler, young wife of Lt. Frederick Dengler. The women chat and during their quick exchange and introductions, Jean mentions her prior work in establishing the fraternity of Chi Omega back in her college town while a student at the University of Arkansas.[1]

## The Founders of Chi Omega

Ina May Boles    Jobelle Holcombe    Dr. Charles Richardson    Alice Cary Simonds    Jean Vincenheller

[Wikipedia]

*(Historical Note: "Founded in 1895 at the University of Arkansas, Chi Omega is the largest women's fraternal organization in the world with over 310,000 initiates and 174 collegiate chapters. Throughout Chi Omega's long and proud history, the Fraternity has brought its members unequaled opportunities for personal growth and development." From Chi Omega web site.)*

[From Chi Omega web site]

Ella welcomes Jean to the neighborhood, and then continues on her way down the path towards the lighthouse.

---

[1] The Army wives stationed along Officers' Row at Fort Rosecrans now become a part of the rich and proud heritage of the Chi Omega legacy, by their association with one of its founding members.

*Fort Rosecrans with Ballast Point Lighthouse and Coronado in the distance.*

*(Historical Note: James Sweet and David Splaine were the lighthouse keepers at Ballast Point Lighthouse during the build-up of the fort. Ballast Point is the strip of land and peninsula adjacent to the fort. James tended to the channel buoys and beacons throughout San Diego Harbor as well. He was also an accomplished violin player who performed at many of the dances held at Roseville Pavilion in nearby La Playa and also at the new post. It was at one of these dances that he met and courted local sweetheart Celia Rogers. In 1904, Celia was a resident of Point Loma and worked as an operator for the Sunset Telephone and Telegraph Company. James and Celia were married on July 4, 1905 at sea on the vessel Point Loma, not far from their lighthouse home.)*

TREASURY DEPARTMENT,                  387

OFFICE OF THE SECRETARY,

Washington,        April 27,1903.

Mr. James R. Sweet,

Care of the Chairman

of the Light-House Board,

Sir:-

You are hereby transferred from the position of First
Assistant Keeper of the Point Sur Light-Station, California,
and appointed Keeper of the San Diego Bay Beacons, California,
with compensation at the rate of $720.00 per year, from
March 26, 1903, subject to taking the required oath of office.

Respectfully,

Acting Secretary.

# SAN DIEGO
## CITY AND COUNTY
# DIRECTORY
### 1904

Rogers Anna, dom Maple nw cor 4th.
Rogers Celia A, opr Sunset Tel and Tel Co, res Point
    Loma.
Rogers Daniel W, driver, res Point Loma.
Rogers Della, clk, bds 2065 Robinson ave.

*Fort Rosecrans*

[Both courtesy of Steve Ruhlen from the Colonel George Ruhlen Family Photo Collection]

*Battery Wilkeson and the Lighthouse on Ballast Point*

*L*ay down your head and close your eyes
and rest your weary soul,
For the lighthouse shines through fog, and rain,
and night as black as coal!

Though winds are lashing and waves are crashing
on coral reefs below,
The beacon calls and beckons all
with its majestic beam aglow.

When stars are out and seas are calm
and eventide draws nigh—
The seafarer rocks in a cradle of waves
to The Lighthouse Lullabye.

*The Lighthouse Lullabye*, anonymous

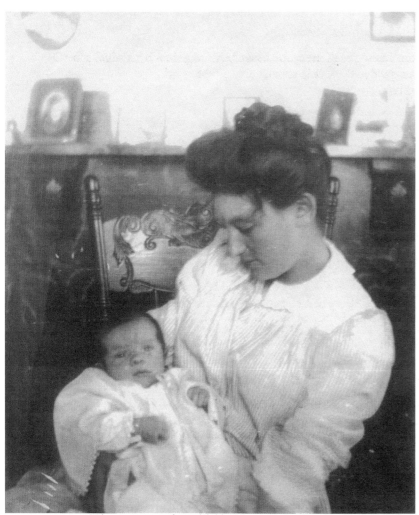

[Photo courtesy of grandchildren James W. Sweet and Janet Sweet Corey]

*At home in the Ballast Point Lighthouse. Celia holding son Alton Relue Sweet, born April 15, 1906, a few days before the San Francisco earthquake.*

SACRED TRUST

[ Courtesy of grandchildren James W. Sweet and Janet Sweet Corey]

*Celia Rogers Sweet walking outside*
*Ballast Point Lighthouse on Cobblestone Point*

[Credit: Summer Evening on the Skagen Southern Beach with Anna Ancher and Marie Kroyer, 1893 (oil on canvas) by Peder Severin Kroyer (1851-1909), Skagens Museum, Denmark/ the Bridgeman Art Library Nationality/copyright status: Danish/out of copyright]

Once again, Ella finds Celia swimming in the ocean by the lighthouse. Celia paddles to the water's edge, unsnaps the strap of her bathing cap under her chin, and says hello to her friend. She plops down on the warm sand, a bit out of breath, and immediately senses by Ella's expression, that something is wrong. Ella confides in her new neighbor that she is upset that her husband has left so soon after their recent move into quarters.

CELIA

But Ella, you knew he was in the Army when you married him. Come now...you and I both know this was to be expected. It just happened a little sooner than you first thought it would, that's all. You can't be mad at him for doing his job. And what are you so worried about anyhow? Jim and I are always right here, just a cobblestone's throw away (they both laugh over the pun regarding their standing on the location of Cobblestone Point), if you should need anything, anything at all, while Ernest is gone. You know you are always welcome at the lighthouse, day or night.

ELLA

I know Celia, you're right.   But I'm not as strong or brave
as you. I don't know how you do it. I will learn from you.
I just thank God everyday that you live out here on the
peninsula too, and close by.

Celia invites her back to the lighthouse cottage for tea, comforts her a bit
more, and gives her a gift. It is a journal and pen set to help her pass the
time while Ernest is away.

When Ella returns to her home, trunks and boxes await her.

But she sits in a chair by the fireplace, by herself, opens her new journal,
and begins to write.

[Fireside. Courtesy of Victorian Trading Company]

**And exactly one hundred years later, Alle Brighton, another new Army wife, sits alone in those same quarters, by that same fireplace, opens Ella's journal, and begins to read...**

ALLE
"I know exactly how you felt Ella."

She admires those early Point Loma "pioneers." Life at the lighthouse and on the Army post must have been rough, rugged, and isolated in so many ways. Only strong-willed, resourceful women could possess the strength and perseverance to overcome the hardships and struggles inherent in their adopted lifestyles. Alle will try to be the same. The lessons in the journal will teach and guide her. She continues reading...

Celia is often seen on the bay ferrying passengers to and from Coronado's Tent City, a beachfront area adjacent to the Hotel del Coronado. It is a favorite destination among local residents, as well as visiting tourists, with its year-round concerts, carousel, and boardwalk entertainment.

It boasts an amusement park atmosphere with fun for old and young alike.

[San Diego History Center]

*Tent City, Coronado, California*

"Ella," yells Celia standing at the top of the lighthouse tower, "hop in the boat and come join me!! I'm going over to Coronado for the day!! Let's have a picnic on the beach! "

[Courtesy of Maritime Museum of San Diego]

*Cobblestone Point, Ballast Point Lighthouse*

The first Christmas season at Fort Rosecrans brings joy to the families living on Officers' Row. The population of San Diego is growing. It is Christmas Eve and everyone is excited to witness the country's first outdoor electric lighting of a living tree. Captain and Mrs. Scott travel by horse-drawn carriage (tally-ho) to the festive event. Ella is wrapped in her new burgundy velvet cape with white fur trim, a warm blanket covering her knees. The resort is cloaked in traditional holiday finery; wreaths, garlands, ribbons, and candles. Christmas carolers stand at the poinsettia-carpeted front entrance and greet the crowd.

Major and Mrs. Rolfe and Major and Mrs. Kneedler converse with military and civic leaders over drinks of cinnamon wassail. The Windsors, Ingles, Engels, and Larsons are all in attendance for the magnificent holiday event. Seeing Mrs. Larson across the room, Ella approaches her to inquire about the whereabouts of Lizzy.

Mrs. Larson pretends not to see her coming, lowers her eyes, and walks briskly in the opposite direction. Ella views her behavior as a little strange and peculiar, but nonchalantly dismisses it, in the spirit of the holiday. She heads to the Hotel's gift shop to buy Lizzy a souvenir of the glorious evening.

*A friend purchased this ornament for me at The Del Gift Shop in 2004.*

By now the Windsor and Engel families have resolved all their differences regarding the marriage of Ella to Ernest, so everyone is more than cordial with one another as they gather around the massive Christmas tree glowing in the hotel lobby. Each year the tree is decorated in a different theme. This Yuletide season, it is brimming with colorful, imported, blown-glass German ornaments. Mrs. Florence von Engel is in her glory, almost to the point of taking credit.

The guests are summoned by the sound of sleigh bells ringing and escorted outside to the front lawn for the historic "electric" lighting of the tree. The branches twinkle on the evergreen and the scent of pine fills the air.

[Photo courtesy of Hotel del Coronado, Heritage Department]

*The country's first outdoor electrically-lighted, living Christmas tree is illuminated on December 24, 1904 at Hotel Del Coronado. The star pine stood on the front lawn at the east end of the Crown Room. It is possible that the families living along Officers' Row enjoyed the sight and historic event during that holiday season.*

## Christmas Rain

Hotel del Coronado, Dec. 25.—A Christmas tree in the open air! A Christmas tree in which birds found shelter for the night; a Christmas tree through which the sea breeze swept; a living, growing tree with its roots embracing Mother Earth and its great branches reaching toward the stars—such is Coronado's tree this year.

The tree selected for honor — one of the three splendid Norfolk Island pines on the plaza, between the hotel and the public library station. It has

**An Unusual Day.**

Seldom has Coronado known such a December 24 as yesterday. It was like a bit of April sent to give greeting at Christmas tide. There were dashes of sunshine, soft breezes blew all day long and at short intervals the sky would become overcast and rain descended.

It is a long time since a Christmas so rich in blessings has been experienced in this region. The grass, trees, vines and lawns have taken on new life and fresh beauty. Already in fancy one beholds wild flowers covering the earth —

# CHRISTMAS RAIN

*San Diego Union*, December 25, 1904

Hotel del Coronado, Dec. 25 – A Christmas tree in the open air! A Christmas tree in which birds found shelter for the night; a Christmas tree through which the sea breeze swept; a living, growing tree with its roots embracing Mother Earth and its great branches reaching toward the stars, such is Coronado's tree this year.

The tree selected for honor is one of the three splendid Norfolk Island pines on the plaza, between the hotel and the public library station. It has attained a height of fifty feet and its branches stand proudly forth.

All day yesterday, electricians were busy fitting it up and by night over 250 lights of many colors gave beauty to the fine old pine. Lanterns great and small, hung from its boughs.

All evening long the radiant tree was the object of admiration. All evening long two barefooted children, a boy and a girl, stood in the shadow of one of the near-by palms and gazed upon the beaming tree. The little girl held her brother's hand close within her own. They spoke scarcely a word.

The imprint of their little feet is even yet visible in the rain softened earth beneath the palm.

When the rain began to come down faster and faster the children, casting a last long look upon the beauty of the night, sped away home to tell of the wonderful Christmas tree. Little wonder that all the children marveled, for their elders did the same, and now that the open-air Christmas tree has been introduced, **it is likely that another Christmas Eve will find many California gardens aglow with light scattered from living foliage.**

The hotel tree will be lighted again tonight from 7 to 10 o'clock, and if it does not rain harder than it did last evening there will no doubt be many to see the electric novelty.

## Today's Concert

All who visit Coronado today on their Christmas outing are cordially invited to attend the concert to be given at the hotel from 3:15 to 4:15 this afternoon in the hotel auditorium. The following selections will be rendered: Grand overture, "Rosamunde" (Shubert); Venetian love song (Nevin); Spanish dances (Moszkowski); waltz suite, "Home of my Childhood" (Ziehrer); grand selection "Pagliacci" (Leoncavolio); "Rose Mouse"(Bosc); march, selected.

## Grill Room Opened

A Christmas Eve supper was given in the pretty new grill room last night at 11 o'clock by Walter H. Dupee and Julius Wangenheim. The rooms on the ocean front formerly used for club-rooms have been changed and refitted until they are now among the most attractive in the big hotel.

Six large windows open to the sea: fine rugs cover the floor; potted palms of choice varieties add much to the attractiveness of the new department and a border of rare ...

## An Unusual Day

Seldom has Coronado known such a December 24 as yesterday. It was like a bit of April sent to give greeting at Christmas tide. There were dashes of sunshine, soft breezes blew all day long and at short intervals the sky would become overcast and rain descended.

It is a long time since a Christmas so rich in blessings has been experienced in this region. The ...trees, vines and lawns have taken on new life and fresh beauty. Already in fancy one beholds wild flowers covering the earth and the fragrance of the dainty sand verbena, which trails close beside the sea, seems again to fill the air. The ice plant will soon be sparkling in the sunshine; poppies need but an invitation to break from the brown earth ere their yellow cups will be gathering in the sunshine. Everywhere there is joy. And the rain came again on Christmas morn!

### HOTEL DEL CORONADO

November 1, 2004

Mary Ellen Cortellini
151 Sylvester Rd
San Diego CA 92106-3581

TEL 619 435 6611
WWW.HOTELDEL.COM

Dear Mary Ellen,

With the holidays just around the corner, we invite you to return to the Hotel del Coronado. There's a lot in store at The Del this season from wonderful Thanksgiving events to a fabulous New Year's Eve bash perfect for finishing out the year.

This December is extra special at The Del, as we celebrate the 100th anniversary of the world's first electrically lighted outdoor tree (at The Del in 1904). In addition to the 50,000 white lights that annually adorn the Victorian Building, on December 1st we will also light the original 1904 tree, located on the resort's front lawn. This event will kick off a month-long calendar of holiday activities, including special children's and family programs, Victorian High Tea and holiday dinners.

We hope you'll be able to join us this holiday season.

### HOTEL DEL CORONADO

Thursday, November 11, 2004

Dear Ms. Mary Cortellini,

Welcome to the Hotel del Coronado. We are looking forward to your visit.

The following number confirms that you have made reservations for one Victorian Guestroom arriving Wednesday, December 1 and departing Thursday, December 2, 2004.

---

**GUEST IDENTIFICATION**

GUEST NAME    CORTELLINI, MARY
ACCOUNT NO.    1158408
ROOM NUMBER    3410
DEPARTURE    12/02/04

GUEST
SIGNATURE _____
This card must be presented when charging to your room account. If lost, please report immediately.

---

[100 Years of Light at The Del © Hotel del Coronado, 2004]

*Invitation to the One Hundred Year Anniversary of the 1904 Lighting of the Tree*
*at the Hotel del Coronado, California*

*I made reservations to stay overnight with San Diego military historian Karen Scanlon and another friend.*

**PRESENT DAY — CHRISTMAS**

Alle is invited by Caroline to attend the one hundred-year anniversary of the lighting of that historic tree. It takes place on Christmas Eve at the Hotel Del Coronado.

Alle is so proud to represent the Fort Rosecrans families who were in attendance a century ago. She participates in their honor. After the ceremony Caroline and Alle decide to splurge on an extravagant meal, feeling deprived by the absence of their husbands during the holiday season. The festive candles, flowers, and glorious decorations lighten their mood and put them in the Christmas spirit.

Once the girls return home that evening, Alle runs to her laptop to check-in for news from Scott. He is happy to report that their Commanding Officer, Captain Ken O'Neil, has returned to Afghanistan after treatment for his injuries. For Alle, the triumphant reunion of the wounded CO with his company of Soldiers is a Christmas miracle.

But as Scott describes the first Christmas in the cold, desolate, mountains of Tora Bora, Alle shivers. The setting is in stark contrast to her candlelit evening at the Hotel del Coronado. She makes herself a cup of hot tea, grabs the next set of pages from Ella's journal, and heads upstairs to bed. There is a chill in the air and she is anxious to dive into the cozy layers of flannel sheets, wool blanket, and down comforter.

As Alle drifts off to sleep, the scene flashes back and we hear Ella's voice again throughout pages of her book...

As the months go by, Ella becomes more confident in fulfilling her role as Commanding Officers' wife at Fort Rosecrans. She is looking forward to entertaining at their beautiful quarters on New Year's Day, a common Army custom at the Post Commander's home. The families living on post gather outside and travel "en masse" to the commandant's house where a festive dinner awaits. All the traditional Army practices are observed; calling cards are given and received, a "holiday programme" amuses and entertains, and the sound of the bugle announces the arrival of the New Year.

Lizzy and Ella break away from some of the festivities to sit and chat in the parlor. Ella is excited to give Lizzy the gift she purchased for her on Christmas Eve at the Hotel Del. She hands the exquisitely wrapped box to Lizzy who tells her she is not feeling well and tears well up in her eyes.

Ella asks, "What's wrong Lizzy? Why are you crying? What is troubling you? You can tell me. You are angry with me for leaving you all these past months, aren't you? Forgive me dear friend, don't be sad."

It is at this moment that Lizzy reveals to Ella that she is pregnant. Ella is shocked to hear the news! When Lizzy discloses that it is Tom's baby she is carrying, Ella is even more stunned by the announcement and flooded with mixed emotions. At first, and to her own surprise, she experiences a strange pang of jealousy. That moment is quickly followed by a feeling of betrayal by both of her childhood friends. But ultimately a sense of overwhelming sympathy and concern for her best friend, and her plight, takes over. She wraps her arms around her and tells her everything will be fine.

Lizzy is inconsolable and shares with Ella that her parents are sending her away to her aunt's home in New York to save the family's good name and standing in the San Diego community. Holding back tears, Ella's heart is breaking for her dear friend. By no fault of her own, Ella feels indirectly responsible and overcome with guilt.

The pageantry of that first New Year's Day celebration in her new home at Fort Rosecrans is overshadowed by the sad news of Lizzy's distressing and unfortunate situation.

## OPENING OF THE NEW BARRACKS AT FORT ROSECRANS

Numerous celebrations wooed society's elite to the doorstep of Fort Rosecrans, but none surpassed the military ball in the new barracks that spring. Major Rolfe, Captain Scott, Post Surgeon Major Kneedler, and their wives hosted naval officers of the Pacific Squadron, who savored an extended port of call at San Diego. A receiving party greeted guests from the flagship *Chicago*, the monitor *Wyoming*, and the revenue cutter *Manning*. But striking among the decorated fellowship was one of the Navy's brightest stars, Commander Lucien Young, Commanding Officer of the patrol gunboat USS *Bennington*. Behind him walks Lieutenant Tom Windsor and Ensign Perry and his new wife who also take their place in the receiving line.

Ella can't help but notice how handsome Tom looks in his formal Navy dress blues. Dictated by the rules of military protocol, he salutes Post Commander Captain Scott. It is an awkward and uncomfortable moment for both men, but a necessary requirement of service etiquette.

Tom takes Ella's hand in his and kisses it gently. Aware that Ernest's eyes are upon him, he holds his grip a little longer. But Ella pulls away, struggling with the knowledge of his unborn child. Angry and hurt, she must maintain her composure until later in the evening when out of the public eye. She is anxious to finally confront him about his past.

A warm fire burned in the huge fireplace. Over its mantel hung two large American flags that crossed each other. Pennants and flags of the various ships were placed throughout the hall. Army officers felt a spirit of pride with the new post, and fitted a large smoking room with divans and easy chairs for the comfort of guests.

*Fort Rosecrans Barracks Building*

[Courtesy of Kim Fahlen, 2004]

A lovely sight is the promenade of swirling gowns along the lengthy porch balcony. The sound of jangling military ornament echoes throughout the halls and across the sparkling waters of the Pacific. When the orchestra begins to play, the guests make their way back inside to the dance floor.

Tom and Ella, however, remain outside and stand motionless, taking the opportunity to converse privately. Ella believes this is her only chance to discuss Lizzy's unfortunate situation and breaks the uncomfortable silence, "I am surprised to see you here tonight Tom. I thought you were leaving the Navy to work at your father's store."

Tom replies, "How could I stay in this city surrounded by so many memories of you and knowing we could never be together? It was too painful to remain here. You gave me no choice Ella. As soon as you departed on your wedding trip, I signed up for another tour of duty on the *Bennington*." Tom adds, "How is life treating you in the Army? I heard you traveled back to San Diego at first without him. Very odd," he says with sarcasm in his voice.

Just when Ella was about to confront him about his tryst with Lizzy, their heated discussion is interrupted by the sound of her husband's voice. He is calling for her from the adjacent room. Ella turns and whispers quietly to Tom, "I have something very important to tell you, meet me out here in one hour." She plans to resume their conversation at that time.

Ernest walks out onto the balcony. He sees the two together, but does not even acknowledge Tom's presence. A bit sternly, Ernest says to his wife, "What are you doing out here? We have official duties to attend to this evening. Let's go back inside."

As Ella turns and walks away following Ernest, Tom yells out to her, "Is this your happily ever after Ella?"

Tom, feeling slighted yet again, slips out of the reception and returns to the ship, without ever saying goodbye to anyone.

The military ball was elegant and festive. Young Ensign Perry danced endlessly with Vipont, his bride of less than two years. Everyone in attendance hated to see the evening end. As the orchestra played their last song, Ella searched the Barracks building for Tom. She knew it was time to divulge the news about Lizzy. It needed to be done. As Ella walked from room to room, she became increasingly agitated. Tom was nowhere to be found.

At the end of the night, Major and Mrs. Rolfe, Major and Mrs. Kneedler and Captain Scott bid farewell to all the honored guests of the Pacific Squadron. Ella was visibly absent. Major Rolfe heartily shook the hand of Commander Lucien Young U.S.N., patting him on the back and wishing him well.

Amidst the protocol and gaiety of the evening, it was inconceivable for the *Bennington*'s skipper to ever imagine the impending tragic fate of his ship and crew.

The paths of these Army and Navy officers would cross again, sooner than expected.

## PRESENT DAY

A Navy SH-60 helicopter crashes in the mountains of Pakistan, bordering Afghanistan. Two pilots and 6 crewmembers down. One of the pilots is Mike Fletcher, Caroline's husband next door. The Commanding Officer of the helicopter squadron asks for backup in the rescue operation. The terrain is unyielding with freezing temperatures. The Army (EOD) Soldiers from Fort Rosecrans are closest in proximity to the crash site and offer their assistance.

Back in quarters in San Diego, Alle is interrupted by frantic knocks on the door. It is Caroline who has come to tell her about Mike's crash overseas. She breaks down as soon as she begins to speak. "Oh, Carrie, No!" says Alle as she puts her arms around her sobbing friend and comforts her. They walk back next door and Alle gets the kids upstairs to bed, sheltering them from their mother's worry and anguish. On their nightstands she views the family photos of Mike with the kids. It is heartbreaking and Alle tries not to think of the unimaginable. She must be strong for her friend. All the families along Officers' Row pull together and prepare for the worst; it's what military families do best in times of crisis.

Thankfully, after a long night's vigil, the news of a rescue in Pakistan finally comes the next morning. Everyone is alive. The sigh of relief is heavy and palpable. The injured pilots and crew head to Landstuhl in Germany for medical treatment.

Alle returns to her quarters, tired and relieved. A feeling of pride comes over her too. She handled herself well under pressure and realizes she is not the same self-centered person who left the cushy life in the city, only a few months before. Who could have ever imagined she would be volunteering with the elderly and giving comfort to other military wives during a time of war. Alle now regrets her "attitude" the days before her husband's deployment. (character transformation almost complete)

After a long nap, Alle escapes once again into the hidden secrets contained in the beloved letters. They usually bring comfort to her, but this time she is shocked to read and learn about the tragic explosion of the USS *Bennington* in San Diego Bay. Alle is overcome with grief as Ella describes the unspeakable horror of the day's events:

[Naval History & Heritage Command]

Out of nowhere, a resonance of terror echoes from the bay. A thunderous blast...

The sound is sickening and clouds of black steam and the scent of death rise over the waterfront. Rolfe, Scott, Kneedler and others make haste to board the General De Russy and race toward town. There's been an explosion aboard the 1710-ton steel, naval gunboat *Bennington*! She's anchored 100 yards off shore and steam hisses from her boilers at a deafening pitch. The concussion from the blast spewed body parts over the length of the ship and into San Diego Harbor. Some dove voluntarily into the water to escape the murderous steam engulfing the ship. On deck sailors lay dead and dying, melting. On the upper deck, they scream and moan. The scene is chaos. Frantic.

Commander Lucien Young who was ashore doing errands when the initial blast occurred, hastens to board the stricken vessel.

On deck, Lieutenant Tom Windsor is slumped against a bulkhead, his uniform practically melted from his body. He is severely scalded but manages still to go below and bring up other survivors. His heroic efforts that day result in the rescue of countless young sailors.

*(Historical Note: Eleven sailors from the USS* Bennington *were awarded the Navy Medal of Honor as a result of their courage and heroism after the explosion July 21, 1905: Oscar Frederick Nelson, Raymond E. Davis, Frank E. Hill, Edward William Boers, William Sidney Shacklette, George F. Brock, William Cronan, John J. Clausey, Rade Grbitch, Emil Fredericksen, Otto Diller Schmidt.)*

On Tom's last attempt, the engine room is aflame. Four men are sprawled on the floor, but it's too late to help them. He has no choice but to return topside where he collapses with exhaustion, and slips overboard.

The government launch eases toward the wreckage and ties up at the foot of the wharf. Captain Scott is first off and dives into the debris-strewn bay, stripped of his shoes and uniform coat. With fierce determination, he begins to rescue bodies who struggle to stay afloat.
One of them is Tom Windsor, blackened and barely conscious. The two men make eye contact with one another. Without hesitation, and straining with outstretched arm, Ernest grabs Tom and pulls him to the surface. He is injured but alive. Many others, not as fortunate, will die in the blood-soaked water alongside the burning wreckage.

Major Rolfe and post surgeon Major Kneedler work tirelessly ashore and begin to move the scorched bodies into a makeshift hospital ward at San Diego Barracks. Major Kneedler and his hospital corpsmen tend to those still breathing, smoke escaping their lungs.

*(Historical Note: Army Officer Captain Scott will ultimately receive a commendation by Charles H. Darling, Acting Secretary of the Navy, for his actions following the disaster.)*

Then, another dull rumbling roar, like distant thunder. Soldiers and sailors freeze in disbelief. Another boiler explodes on the crippled ship. The whole deck seems to lift. Windows rattle throughout the town.

Onlookers from shore shake themselves into action. Some assist in the delivery of bodies to funeral homes or local hospitals. Citizens comb the streets in horse-drawn buggy giving food and drink, blankets, and comfort.

From Ballast Point, Celia can see the black smoke rising over the harbor. She yells for Ella, "Something terrible has happened! Quick, jump in the boat! We must go and help! Hurry!"

Celia and Ella quickly make their way to the downtown waterfront area hoping they'll find survivors. Captain Scott directs the two young women to the old barracks building where they are pressed into service setting up cots and comforting the injured. Ensign Perry is there having survived the blast, only to die hours later.

Ella, nauseated by the stench of singed flesh, is overwhelmed and afraid. She moves beyond the row of beds for a moment, apart from the bustle of activity, and begins to cry.

From somewhere, a voice reaches out to her. Familiar. Weak... " Ella."

Ella stifles her tears and attends to the call of a battered, injured figure lying on a cot. He's barely recognizable. In his last remaining moments he utters the words,

"Ella, he is worthy of you. He is your happily ever after."

These are the last words spoken by this young officer before he expires.

**Ella falls to her knees and lowers her head onto the chest of Tom Windsor and weeps uncontrollably. "You have a child Tom. You are a father." But the words come too late.**

Three days following the disaster, a mass burial service for forty-seven of the victims is held at the Post Cemetery, on the hill above Officers' Row.

The coffins are laid in a single, large grave. An Army Lieutenant from Fort Rosecrans receives each one and arranges an identifying name board, for future headstones.

A large crowd of soldiers, sailors, and townspeople gather and Commander Young addresses the funeral crowd, saying,

> "Captain Scott and officers and successors at Fort Rosecrans, I want to commit to your tender care the bodies of our unfortunate shipmates and patriotic dead. May their graves never be forgotten by the hand of affection, and may marble slabs rise on this, their last earthly resting place, and may the morning and evening sun playing upon the grassy mounds, be symbolical of their shipmates' affection.

> Captain Scott replies: "I accept the Sacred Trust of the honored dead."

Under her breath, Ella repeats the same words..."I too accept the Sacred Trust of the honored dead."

Then comes the command in sharp tones from the sergeant in charge of the artillery company. "Attention!" he calls. Guns point over the long rows of caskets. Three sharp volleys ring out over the bay. Out of the ranks steps a bugler and taps are sounded. The crowd turns and walks away. And it is over.

Newspapers throughout the nation carry the news of the disaster and President Theodore Roosevelt himself sends his expression of sympathy. Lizzy reads the headlines in New York about the tragedy and faints upon hearing the news of Tom's death by telegram. In her fragile condition she is rushed to the hospital and goes into labor brought on by the shock. Hours later, that same evening, she gives birth to a little girl. The baby is named Elizabeth, same name as her mother, as was common practice in those days. Lizzy summons Ella to come to New York as soon as possible.

## NEXT SCENE — ELIZABETH'S HOME IN NEW YORK

Ella travels by train cross-country to be at her friend's side in her time of need and to attend the child's christening. Lizzy has asked her to be the godmother. When she sees the baby for the first time, asleep in her cradle, her resemblance to Tom is overwhelming. Ella is overcome with grief and sorrow. She breaks down and weeps.

**Then she removes the glittering locket from her purse, breaks it in two, and pins the "E" half of it to the baby's christening gown.**

Under her breath she whispers, "A gift from the father you will never know. He was a good man. He died a hero in San Diego. His only mistake in life was loving me. It is because of my refusal to marry him that he returned to duty on the ill-fated *Bennington*. Now he is gone. Forever. It is all my fault. If only I could go back in time and right the wrong that has occurred. I loved him to the depths of my soul. But it was not the kind of love he longed for, and needed, from me. If only he had known about you, things would have been so different. Forgive me my dear Elizabeth. In your lifetime, you will learn the truth. It is my "Sacred Trust" to him, and to you.

One hundred years later, that "Sacred Trust" will be complete...

## PRESENT DAY

Alle now realizes that the modern-day soldiers of Fort Rosecrans are the successors mentioned at the original Memorial Service for the *Bennington* sailors a century ago. It is a profound discovery revealed to her in Ella's writings.

She is anxious to share this unbelievable information about the USS *Bennington* with her friend on Coronado. But for the first time ever, the elderly woman doesn't keep the appointment. Alle is deeply concerned. She runs across the street to the library, grabs a local phone book sitting on the counter, and looks up Elizabeth's home address. When Alle arrives at her house on Adella Ave, the bronze plaque by the front door catches her eye. Apparently the building has recently been registered as a Coronado Historical Landmark. A nurse comes to the front door and escorts her upstairs. She tells her that Elizabeth had been rushed to Coronado Hospital the night before with some minor chest pain. She was discharged earlier that morning and returned home without incident, or cause for further concern. Alle finds her resting comfortably in bed. Elizabeth apologizes to Alle for missing their scheduled meeting.

"Absolutely no apology necessary," says Alle as she fluffs the patients pillow and pours her some tea, "are you up for another reading today?" Elizabeth emphatically answers in the affirmative.

"I must warn you however," replies Alle, "that the news from the journal, not unlike your condition today, is less than cheerful."

As Alle shares the stories about the *Bennington* disaster, Elizabeth stops and interrupts her for a moment and motions to Alle to bring a little box sitting on her dresser. On the outside there is a painting of a sparkling Christmas tree at the Hotel del Coronado. Inside contains a yellowed and deteriorating old newspaper article. The headlines report, "USS *Bennington* Explodes in San Diego Bay."

Then Alle continues the story ... including the military funeral and Ella's subsequent trip to see the new baby after the disaster...

Elizabeth grows increasingly pale. The old woman is visibly shaken and gasps for air. Alle assumes that it must be her heart again. But then, very slowly and deliberately, Elizabeth pulls a necklace out from beneath her nightgown. Attached to the chain is a small round piece of gold with the initial "E" engraved on it.

Putting all of the pieces of the puzzle together, including the contents of her mother's souvenir box, Elizabeth now knows the identity of her father!! Tom Windsor, Naval Officer, of the USS *Bennington*.

Alle's head is spinning! She too begins to put the pieces together and now understands her and Elizabeth's connection to the first group of soldiers stationed at Fort Rosecrans. And the magnitude of the realization overwhelms her. She was put in Ella's house on Officers' Row for a reason. The unbelievable parallels in her own life with Scott are not just a coincidence!!

**Ella's letters are a message from the grave. She has been trying to warn Alle and save her from the same heartbreak.**

The clock is ticking now. Time is running out to stop the disastrous repetition of the past and its fatal outcome. Alle must save her husband! But how? He is on the other side of the world, millions of miles away from her!!

| DRAMATIC SCENE OF THE FATAL INCIDENT WHICH OCCURRED IN AFGHANISTAN APRIL 15, 2002 |
|---|

*(SSG Jeff Pugmire was the only survivor of the explosion which took the lives of three Fort Rosecrans soldiers and one Special Forces medic. This scene will be based on SSG Pugmire's powerful, poignant, and heart wrenching account of that tragic event. It will serve to educate the American people about the brutality and ruthlessness of our enemy overseas and highlight the importance of our military and the need to be vigilant in the ongoing war on terror.)*

Back in Afghanistan the unit is tasked with clearing all of the ordnance surrounding Kandahar Air Field, now U.S. Headquarters. This area includes "Ammo Valley," a 12 mile stretch of littered weapons, left by the Taliban.

Captain Scott Brighton along with his three buddies Jake, Bill, and Toby and a Special Forces medic named Dan, walk towards a booby-trapped cache.

As the men work together to stack mounds of ordnance for disposal, Scott leans over and a shiny gold object falls out of his uniform pocket. At the same moment that he bends to pick it up, an explosion occurs that will take the lives of his four friends out there in the field. He is the only survivor. His close friends Jake, Bill, and Toby from the 710th and the SF medic, are killed instantly by the blast. Reaching for the broken half of the locket with the letter "T" engraved on it, saved Scott's life.

Mike Fletcher's squadron hears about the explosion on the radio and they are immediately called in for medevac. By the time Mike gets there, Scott is barely alive. He transports the lone survivor by helicopter to the nearest military medical facility for emergency surgery.

Now it will be Alle who relies on the friendship of the military family support groups in her time of need.

Scott, seriously wounded, flies home to the United States in a C-130. He is unaware that the transport plane is also carrying the remains of his fallen comrades. The other men from the 710th who accompany him home, conceal this information from him, and salute the flag-covered caskets as they are unloaded from the plane.

*Memorial Service which took place at Naval Base Point Loma, April 19, 2002.*

Despite his injuries, Scott gives the eulogy for his three close friends at the Memorial Service at Fort Rosecrans National Cemetery. It is the hardest thing he's ever had to do. The pain in the faces of the Army wives and their children is excruciating. The horrors of war will haunt him the rest of his life.

Captain Scott Brighton calls on the people of San Diego to never forget the Soldiers of Fort Rosecrans, their "hometown boys" killed in the line of duty. They gave their lives for their country. They were men of honor.

Scott is medically discharged from the Army. He and Alle are forever changed by the revelation of the historic events of the past and the tragic events which took place in Afghanistan.

(*Historical Note: Heroism of Army personnel stationed at Fort Rosecrans after the* Bennington *explosion and the heroism of Army personnel stationed at Fort Rosecrans after the explosion in Afghanistan.*)

Scott and Alle are not the same people who left the city soon after 9/11 and they reluctantly resume their life on Wall Street.

**But the tale does not end here. There is one more thing that Alle must do. She knows that it will be up to her to finish Ella's story — to honor the promise made so many years before between the U.S. Navy and U.S. Army, as revealed in the historic old writings.**

(Alle's character transformation is complete.)

## THE FINAL SCENE — 2005

The story and film come "full circle" when Alle arranges for Scott to fly back to San Diego from New York for a surprise reunion with his buddies in the 710th Ord Co (EOD). Scott hasn't seen most of them since the loss of their comrades that fatal day in Kandahar. Alle invites the Army families who lost loved ones, her former neighbors Caroline and Mike Fletcher, and Elizabeth Fairchild. The tribute will also be in honor of Elizabeth's 100th birthday.

The event takes place at the *Bennington* Monument, an impressive and commanding granite obelisk, within Fort Rosecrans National Cemetery. The setting is breathtaking at the top of Point Loma, overlooking the Pacific Ocean.

The Soldiers assemble in Class A uniforms, standing in formation among the white tombstones, to honor their fallen comrades killed in the explosion in Afghanistan, as well as the sailors who perished in the explosion in San Diego Bay, a century earlier.

Then ... unexpectedly, suddenly, and without warning, it happens ... Captain Scott Brighton arrives in uniform and walks up the grassy hill to take his place in the line-up. It is a reunion of indescribable emotion!! With enormous smiles and overflowing hearts, the "band of brothers" shake hands, and then embrace. It is a moment in time that will last forever. Silent, reverent, patriotic, and joyful.

The words of Commander Lucien Young U.S.N. are heard in the background once again, "Officers and successors at Fort Rosecrans, I want to commit to your tender care....and may their graves never be forgotten by the hand of affection." The event fulfills the promise made between the U.S. Navy and U.S. Army one hundred years ago that day.

*(Historical Note: Surprise reunion of SSG Jeff Pugmire with his former members of his unit as they stood in formation at the base of the* Bennington *Monument to honor the one hundred year old promise. See Epilogue.)*

By the side of the sea and the harbor bar
Where the white breakers roar and run,
That each generation, as years come and go,
Will remember the ship Bennington.

Mrs. E.W. Bour

[Photo by Kim Fahlen]

The Modern-Day Fort Rosecrans Soldiers lined up at the base of the Monument in 2005.

The words spoken by Commander Lucien Young at the military funeral in 1905:

"Captain Scott and officers and successors at Fort Rosecrans, I want to commit to your tender care the bodies of our unfortunate shipmates and patriotic dead. May their graves never be forgotten by the hand of affection ..."

Elizabeth, frail and in a wheelchair now, stares at her father's gravesite with tears of happiness in her eyes. The front of the headstone is engraved with a small cross, the Medal of Honor symbol, and the words:

Thomas Windsor

Medal of Honor

Lt

US Navy

USS *Bennington*

July 21, 1905

The back reads, "A courageous man who died valiantly trying to save his shipmates."

Elizabeth's life slips away peacefully and a vision of her father, with outstretched hand, appears.

Elizabeth is transformed and the same little girl in the pink silk dress and large bow in her hair, from the opening scene of the movie, rises from the chair and reaches for her father.

And as they walk off together hand in hand....

We hear Ella's voice for the last time...disappearing...fading....while at the same time, blending with Alle's saying,

"I too accept the Sacred Trust of the Honored Dead."

# The End

Section 60

The final shot of the film before the closing credits, is a picture of the common gravesite, located at Arlington National Cemetery, for the three Soldiers of the 710th Ordnance Company (EOD) and Special Forces Medic SFC Daniel A. Romero and the words...

In Memory of Fort Rosecrans Soldiers

SSG Justin J. Galewski
SSG Brian T. Craig
SGT Jamie O. Maugans

Killed in Action
April 15, 2002
Operation Enduring Freedom

Epilogue

*(Historical Note: Captain Robert Henry Rolfe and Captain Ernest Darius Scott transferred from Fort Rosecrans in August 1905. Both men continued their distinguished Army careers serving in World War I and beyond. Rolfe retired by law at age 64, achieving the rank of Colonel. Scott culminated his career as a highly decorated Brigadier General. Their legacy remains in San Diego. One hundred years later, eight of the fourteen original buildings stand in historic preservation.)*

Visual of actual headstones found at Arlington National Cemetery in honor of Brigadier General Ernest D. Scott and his wife Ella, Colonel Robert H. Rolfe and his wife Grace, and at Laurel Hill Cemetery in Philadelphia for Major William L. Kneedler and his wife Lydia.

[Arlington National Cemetery]

Brigadier General and Mrs. Ernest D. Scott

[Both Arlington National Cemetery]

Colonel and Mrs. Robert H. Rolfe      Section 3  1860A

*Major Kneedler is buried at Laurel Hill Cemetery in Philadelphia, Pennsylvania*
*The cemetery is a Registered National Historic Landmark*

*Fort Rosecrans Post Surgeon*

[Photo courtesy of Mrs. Lenore Morton]

# 710th Ordnance Company honors Army-Navy promise

By Karen Scanlon and Mary Ellen Cortellini

It was business as usual along San Diego's waterfront in the early morning of July 21, 1905. But a boiler explosion at 10:33 a.m. aboard the patrol gunboat USS *Bennington* plundered the ordinary and remains one of the deadliest peacetime disasters in the history of the Navy.

Bennington's highly-decorated skipper, Cmdr. Lucien Young, ordered steam up for a noon departure on that fateful Friday and then walked to town on ship's business.

Crews, who had anticipated liberties in San Diego, grudgingly threw coal into *Bennington's* hungry furnaces. Instead, they were ordered north to tow an ailing squadron mate, USS *Wyoming*.

Topside, they were busy sweeping coal dust from the deck of the warship after 300 tons of "black diamonds" had been admitted to her bunkers. For two hours coal passers fed the furnaces, but the steam-pressure gauge showed nothing. Steam shot out of cracks in the boiler, but the gauge registered zero.

Suspicious, they sent a fireman above for a trouble-shooting engineer. All of them ignorant that someone had incorrectly closed an air cock, stopping the passage of steam to the pressure gauge. The gang threw on more coal.

Army Constructing Quartermaster Capt. Robert Henry Rolfe was returning by launch from Fort Rosecrans to his office across the bay. The build-up of the permanent post on Point Loma was just finished and a post commander assigned—West Point graduate, Capt. Ernest Darius Scott.

As Rolfe steamed toward town, a low, rumbling roar caught his attention. Then, two, quick blasts!

"It was the gunboat *Bennington* exploding before my very eyes," he later told a reporter. "The whole deck seemed to lift."

Clouds of black steam and the scent of death rose over the waterfront. *Bennington* shuddered and steam hissed from her boilers at deafening pitch, filling every compartment. The concussion from the blasts spewed body parts over the length of the ship and into the bay.

Rolfe boarded the 1,710-ton steel wreck. He witnessed men ripping at their uniforms and diving to escape the clouds engulfing the warship. Sailors scrambled from below.

Staff Sgt. Jeff Pugmire (right) greets members of his former unit at a ceremony at the Bennington Monument
Photo by Kim Fahlen

On deck, lay the dead and dying.

The blast was so devastating, the ship began to list to the starboard side. A tug boat was steered alongside. Chief Boatswain's Mate Lyn Gauthier caught sight of it from a port window and helped secure the lines. He quickly realized the ship couldn't be towed with its anchor resting on the bay floor.

Gauthier grabbed a fire ax and fought his way to the chain locker below. He cut away the manila lashings of the anchor chain's "bitter end" and freed the ship for movement by tug into the shallows of San Diego Bay. His efforts prevented the ship from sinking and carrying stunned survivors to a watery grave. Sadly, Gauthier died the next day, his lungs scorched.

USS *Bennington* boasted an intimidating armament and an officer on board ordered the magazine flooded. Chief Gunner's Mate John Clausey dashed below to open the flood valves. He was one of 11 to receive the Navy Medal of Honor.

On shore and off, horrified onlookers shook themselves into action. Mariners swept the bay for the injured and dead. One reporter wrote, "It is awfully indescribable…the brave boys with faces and hands torn and lacerated, their clothing stripped from their backs, burned and blackened."

See "Ordnance," page 9

---

From "Ordnance," page 8

Citizens and businesses offered what comfort they could. Undertakers competed at the barge wharf. And a death march of hacks and wagons of every description delivered bodies to local mortuaries or to the city's two hospitals.

Scott opened the old quarters near the waterfront as an auxiliary medical facility.

In charge was the post surgeon at Fort Rosecrans, Maj. William Ludwig Kneedler—the first medical man to board the vessel. His team of Army medical corpsmen worked for six days, until more help arrived.

In all, 64 enlisted sailors and one officer died in the explosion. Many more of the ship's crew of 197 were critically injured.

Citizens, military personnel, and able *Bennington* survivors ascended the hill to the Post Cemetery above Fort Rosecrans for a mass funeral on July 23. Forty-seven coffins were laid in a single, large grave.

Lt. William Tobin received each coffin and arranged an identifying name board, for future headstones. Clergy spoke and blessed the sailors.

Then, Bennington's captain, Cdr. Young addressed the funeral crowd, saying, "Scott and officers and successors at Fort Rosecrans, I want to commit to your tender care the bodies of our unfortunate shipmates… May their graves never be forgotten by the hand of affection."

Scott replied, "I accept the sacred trust of the honored dead."

In that moment, he commenced their care on behalf of generations to come.

To mark the centennial of the *Bennington* explosion, the authors arranged a military tribute with the contemporary Army suc-

cessors—the 710th Ordnance Company —attached to the former Fort Rosecrans.

It made sense to invite the 710th to stand at the Bennington Monument and "lay the hand of affection" upon the sailors. Thus, honoring the promise made long ago between the Army and Navy.

The Soldiers also stood to honor their own.

Following 9/11, George W. Bush sent a Presidential directive of the highest priority to the Soldiers. In a month, they were deployed to Afghanistan. Their mission: to discover the extent of the Al Qaeda weapons of mass destruction and support U.S. intelligence agencies. They diffuse bombs.

"At the time, Afghanistan was the most dangerous place in the world," says Staff Sgt. Raymond Ertle, "with all the land mines and ordnance the Russians had left behind (following a Soviet invasion during the Cold War). When it was time to go, they dropped what they were doing and ran for the border." The leftover weapons were now being used by the Taliban against U.S. troops.

In Jan. 2002, the unit was ordered to

The USS Bennington following the explosion in July 1905.
Courtesy photo

Kandahar. Soldiers destroyed more than 200,000 pieces of hazardous ordnance, conducted 200 combat missions, and eliminated over 100 Taliban and Al Qaeda weapons caches that threatened coalition forces and Afghan citizens.

Their success, however, was at great cost. The lives of three 710th EOD Soldiers—Staff Sgt. Justin J. Galewski, Staff Sgt. Brian T. Craig, and Sgt. Jamie O. Maugans—and 19th Army Special Forces medic, Sgt. 1st Class Aaron Daniel Romero.

One Soldier survived, though badly injured, when the five worked in teams to stack and destroy ordnance in an area known as Ammo Valley. They were "mopping up" a large stash of ammunition that had been scattered across 30 miles of colorless desert valley.

Staff Sgt. Jeff Pugmire was handed a rocket and positioned it on the pile. "As I stood back up, I realized I had put two warheads in the same direction," said Pugmire. "Looking back, I think it's probably what saved my life."

He picked up the rocket again, spun it around, and as the rocket touched the pile, "There was a big, loud boom. Now I'm face down in the sand, 30 feet from where I had been standing." His ears were ringing, and the world was spinning.

Blood oozed from his body, and pain seared his concentration. And then, that slow- motion sense. "I saw body pieces. There should be four more Americans here, I said to myself." But they were gone.

An investigation identified that it had not been the rocket Pugmire repositioned on the stack that exploded. Instead, his comrades worked in the hot sun standing over a booby-trapped ordnance cache, left for them by the Taliban.

Pugmire is medically retired from the Army now and lives in Oregon. We flew him to San Diego to surprise his 710th EOD comrades. And a surprise it was!

Cameras were poised on the smart stance of the Soldiers in standard Army Class A uniforms. "Wait, there's one more Soldier coming!" we announced.

Ertle said later, that he looked down the line to both sides to see who was missing. "I mentally counted, we were all here?"

Then up over the grassy mound appeared Pugmire. It seems not one Soldier knew what to do. So they stood firm, obviously anxious to break away.

What followed was something very special—like loved ones coming together after a long separation.

As the Soldiers left the cemetery that gray March morning, Ertle and Pugmire stood side-by-side facing the Bennington Monument. Their military resolve unshaken. "Present arms!" Ertle called. And a venerable salute was rendered.

[John Wagstaffe, Public Affairs Office, Fort Irwin, National Training Center]

**Surprise reunion of only survivor of 710th incident in Afghanistan.**

## The Soldiers of the 710th Ordnance Company (EOD)
## Honoring the Promise a Century Later in 2005

[Photo by Kim Fahlen]

### In Remembrance—Army Soldiers at Navy Graves

The ship's commanding officer asked that the post commander and successors at Fort Rosecrans remember his shipmates. A century later the Soldiers of the 710th Ordnance Company (Explosive Ordnance Disposal) are the successors.

Soldiers of the 710th ORD CO (EOD) attached to Army-built, former Fort Rosecrans (Naval Base Point Loma today) stand at the graves of *Bennington* sailors to honor the promise made between the U.S. Navy and the U.S. Army.

August 2006

Pitch letter sent to Producers and Directors:

I would love to set up a meeting to discuss my Screenplay Proposal for a future film called Sacred Trust, based on my story "The Forgotten Soldiers of Fort Rosecrans." As a Navy Captain's wife, and during the course of five years of historical research living on the former Army post, I have brought the first occupants of Officers' Row back to life during its heyday. Sifting through reels of microfilm at the library, I learned that the 'characters' are inextricably woven throughout the wonderful social and military events that took place in San Diego over a century ago. The setting overlooking San Diego Bay, Coronado, and the Pacific Ocean is breathtaking. There were military balls at the famous seaside resort Hotel del Coronado, picnics atop the cliffs of Point Loma, parades along Fifth Ave, and fireworks over Glorietta Bay. The plot includes a love story between the handsome West Point graduate, Captain E. D. Scott, and the local daughter of high society, Ella von Gerichten. It highlights the beauty, elegance, and military pageantry in the city at the turn of the 20th century. Scenes take place along the San Diego waterfront, the historic Gaslamp District, the Ballast Point Lighthouse, and the Coast Artillery installation of Fort Rosecrans. There are booming guns, daily bugle calls, drills, inspections, and parade formations at the entrance to San Diego Harbor.

However, there is also a contemporary twist; the story line about the modern-day Fort Rosecrans Soldiers stationed on the former post, one hundred years later. They are the brave, young members of the 710th Ordnance Company Explosive Ordnance Disposal (EOD), tucked away in the old post bakery building.

Personal interviews I've obtained from the Soldiers provide a rare glimpse into the elite and dangerous world of Army bomb techs and the families who stand by them. I love these guys, we've all become friends, and I can't wait for you to meet them. They are amazing! By honoring the three fallen Soldiers from Fort Rosecrans, we will honor all in the Army EOD community. That is our mission and ultimate goal.

This inspirational film will illustrate the bygone era of Army glory in San Diego a century ago and link it to the present war on terror fought by Soldiers of the 710th today. It's a winning combination! It will appeal to a large audience of men, women, and all those who wear the uniform around the globe.

There has never been a movie produced about the Army in the "Navy town of San Diego" or the exclusive Army EOD community in general, so it is a unique opportunity that is long overdue. I hope you can be a part of this worthwhile project. Thank you!

An Army of One, Plus One
Mary Ellen Cortellini

April 15, 2007

Thanks to Drew Schunk, Regional Vice-President for Lincoln Military Housing, a Monument to Fort Rosecrans Soldiers, past and present, now stands at 1895 Tattnal Way. Open to the public, the Memorial is located along Harbor Drive in San Diego, within Lincoln Military Housing at Liberty Station. It was dedicated in April 2007 on the Fifth Year Anniversary weekend of the loss of the men from the 710th Ord Co (EOD) in Afghanistan.

Memorial Day Weekend, 2007

*My dear friend Karen Scanlon contributed extensive time and talent to this project between 2003-2005.*

*She had a unique ability to turn historical documentation into well-written prose.*

*This book would never have happened without her contributions.*

*After Karen returned to teaching, I continued on with the project.*

*I developed the story line to create the screenplay proposal in this book.*

*The characters of Alle and Scott Brighton, Caroline and Mike Fletcher,*

*Lizzy Larson, Ensign Tom Windsor, and Elizabeth Fairchild are fictional.*

*The name Ella von Gerichten was changed to Ella von Engel for purposes of the screenplay.*

*A number of production companies were contacted, but unfortunately none picked up the film idea.*

*So I decided to publish the story in book form instead.*

*I hope you've enjoyed my fictional interpretation of a tale*

*that has been hidden and laying dormant for over one hundred years.*

## SAN DIEGO FILM COMMISSION

Dear Mary Ellen,                                                                                       December 3, 2009

It was wonderful to have a conversation with you about shooting your film, SACRED TRUST, in San Diego. San Diego wants your business and the Film Commission is committed to your success. While major motion pictures such as *Almost Famous, Traffic, Antwone Fisher,* and *Bring It On,* have chosen to shoot on location in San Diego, our value is often a well-kept secret even in our own back yard of Hollywood and LA. As independent films have become more main stream, there has been an explosion of filmmaking activity over the past few years as producers see the advantage to filming in an area that has a fresh face and a fresh attitude. San Diego brings tremendous production value found in a wealth of untapped locations, amazing natural light and an established infrastructure of local people and resources. But what about the costs?

To begin with, there are NO PERMIT FEES to film in the City of San Diego, in the unincorporated areas of the County or on Port District property. We work very hard to keep public properties free locations so there is no cost to film on a street, sidewalk, beach or parkland. We do practice "cost recovery" so if you need a custodian, ranger, lifeguard or police you would pay for that person's time with no additional overhead or administrative fees. On average, that means I can save you a minimum of $450/day, the cost of a permit application fee in LA, and often thousands of dollars in actual permit costs. We offer a Hotel Discount Program where participating hotels offer at least a 15% room rate discount and often much more depending on time of year and occupancy. We have a deep talent pool of expert technicians and experienced actors. Using local resources will help your budget.

Most importantly, San Diego is a major character in your script. SACRED TRUST is dedicated to the legacy of the military presence in San Diego and the amazing partnership this city, its citizens, communities and the men and women of the armed forces have fostered for over a century. Your story takes place in the landmark areas of Pt. Loma, the Gaslamp Quarter and San Diego Bay; icon locations that are preserved in their importance today. You cannot make this movie any place other than San Diego! The pride we take in the stories of our fallen heroes, along with the support of the military, local governments and all of San Diego at large guarantees your movie will be seen on the big screen. The Film Commission is here for you to provide hands-on assistance, to facilitate all permits, and act as liaison to guarantee your success. We welcome you and SACRED TRUST to San Diego's back lot.

Best regards,


Kathy M. McCurdy
Director of Features

(619) 234-FILM, Fax: (619) 234-4631, www.sdfilm.com
1010 Second Avenue. Suite 1500. San Diego. California 92101

SACRED TRUST                                                                                                    113

If my dreams could all come true —
Paradise would be —

— In a little bungalow —

Somewhere ....

.... By the sea.          D. Morgan © 1993

[D. Morgan, © 1993]

## About the Author

## Mary Ellen Cortellini

Mary Ellen Cortellini graduated in 1980 from the College of the Holy Cross, Worcester, Massachusetts. She is married to Captain Louis Cortellini, USN (Ret.), former Commodore of HSCWINGPAC (Helicopter Anti-Submarine Wing, U.S. Pacific Fleet), NAS North Island, San Diego. She is the proud mother of one daughter, Christine, born in Coronado, CA, a graduate of Boston College with a Masters Degree in Education, and kindergarten teacher at La Jolla Country Day School, La Jolla, California. As a 27-year "career" Navy wife and Commanding Officer's spouse in three different commands, Mary Ellen was always active in Officer and Enlisted Spouses' Clubs. In 2007 a Monument to Fort Rosecrans Soldiers, past and present, was dedicated in San Diego based on the research she had undertaken as a resident of the former post. This book is the third in the author's series based on San Diego's rich military history.

11072313R00066

Made in the USA
San Bernardino, CA
07 May 2014